Nil Desperandum

Chapters

1	Today, Piranhas
2	2018, Paraparaumu
3	2004, Mansfield
4	'97, Marylebone
5	'96, Kawasaki
6	'95, Davy Crockett
7	'94, AK-47
8	'92, Purple urn
9	'90, Porky and Scarface
10	'80s, Saudis
11	'80s, Luton Airport Parkway
12	'80s, West African coast guard
13	'83, The Hackney Rock
14	'83, Fingered by Leonard
15	'79, Hitler is a little shit
16	'77, Racing for Holland
17	'77, Hotdog
18	'76, Sally
19	'75, Roman numerals joke
20	'75, 12p
21	'71, The Welsh language Liverpool Daily Echo
22	'67, Buggy
23	'60s, Skip Barber's pit stop
24	'60s, Burlington Arcade
25	'64, The Movie Scene
26	'64, Sheffield Telegraph
27	'63, The Mountain
28	'63, Two Nuns
29	'63, Lion tamer or astronaut or something
30	'63, Ungentlemanly
31	'62, SEXI
32	'62, OOO
33	'62, Suits you
34	'62, Cooper
35	'50s, Milk float
36	'50s, Arthur Longbottom
37	'50s, Taters
38	'52, Sir Baz
39	'47, A driver and a carman

Chapter 1 – Today, Piranhas

I recall the excitement of sitting down to watch the '97 film Titanic with an elderly relative, volume turned right up, and as the ship set sail they thoughtfully remarked, 'It sinks at the end, y'know.' Thanks for that. That timely fact has saved me from having to watch the rest of the film. And so I'll share a Titanic moment with you now – Roy James is dead. When I started researching this book about him, I was helpfully told this fact, as well as two other facts; Roy James was the racing driver who made a trophy for Bernie Ecclestone and Roy James was one of the great train robbers. I am grateful for these facts again and again, thanks. Sometimes, depending on who was telling me, Bernie Ecclestone was somehow involved in the robbery. This 'fact' was sometimes backed up with the line that Bernie once playfully told a journo about there not being enough money on the train for him to rob it and, therefore, this denial must mean he's covering something up. And we know Roy was one of the train robbers because he did over ten years in jail for it. But thanks for telling me.

Actually, I should be less ungrateful for information because finding any facts about a secretive man who led a particularly colourful life has proven to be rather difficult. Perhaps that's why no one has written a book about him before. His death in '97 went unnoticed by many, but not me. I'd noticed it in the obituaries section of The Independent, which I was reading as an alternative to the film with its spoiled ending. 'And they all drown, too.' Roy 'The Weasel' James is dead, but his life was far less predictable.

Knowing Roy is dead so early in a book about trying to discover who he really was helps to eliminate some other suspects of the same name. Ours is not the Aussie rules player from a century ago, the Welsh Ironman competitor or 'Bobby Slowik's Nephew' called James Roy on Twitter. That last Roy James is some American sports commentator on Twitter with a verified tick thing. I messaged him to ask if he'd ever robbed a train. I didn't ask him who Bobby Slowik is as it seemed like I should know already. I'm not arsed with social media. A police friend who served in the Met years ago, perhaps tired of me asking him for help with my research, suggested 'try Facebook'. I am not on Facebook. I can confirm that our Roy James is not James Roy the decorated Kiwi soldier nor James Roy the US airman.

If he was famous enough to be listed on Wikipedia, then, on the list of famous people with the same surname as him, he'd fit awkwardly between Robert James (linebacker) and Sally James (Tiswas host). His Christian name comes from the French meaning royal and the phrase 'Le Roy le veult' ('The King wills it') is still used in UK Parliament today. There are 92 people with the surname James listed in the London phone book, which tells me that (a) nobody bothers with the phone book any more and (b) I'm going to have to uncover the Weasel the hard way. So we start in the present day.

In 2023, a smart, detached house was advertised for sale in a place I was asked not to name. The details show the home of what you'd imagine to be an elderly person. There's a painting of a horse on one wall and the gardens are pretty. It's a lovely house with great views. There are some energy-saving features and the owner had the place built to their specification decades ago. The selling agent notes that 'the property flows naturally from room to room', as opposed to flowing unnaturally, I suppose. Perhaps their other properties have molten hot lava in lieu of a connection between rooms or piranha-infested pools requiring inhabitants to leap about Bond-style to avoid getting savaged. To be fair to the agent, they refrain from describing the house in the fashion of most pointy-shoed gits, avoiding 'nestled', 'ever-popular' and the utterly contradictory 'link detached'. Anyway, it's a nice house.

On one wall of this house is a large, framed picture of a single-seat, shark-nosed racing car cornering hard. On the picture is a large, single initial representing the house owner's first name. This, to me, was evidence enough that the house belongs (for now) to 'name removed at their request'. I called the agent and, in his excitement to sell me the place, before I could get a word in edgeways or ask about the naturally flowing layout or caution him about GDPR, blurts out that the house, indeed, belongs to 'name removed at their request'. I'm not interested in buying the house, but I am interested in the inhabitant because 'name' has a connection to our protagonist, Roy James.

This book is about the search for the real Roy James and writing a conventional biography in chronological order would be an anticlimax. We already know he's dead and that he was a great train robber who made a trophy for Bernie, just as surely as icebergs and ships are a bad mix. So my thinking was to work backwards through his life to try and find out who he really was. What happened in his life that put him in an early grave, after having robbed trains and made trophies and stuff? I have not written a biography before, my qualifications being pratting about with old cars and writing for magazines that mostly go bust. So it's easier to start at the end and work backwards, which is more of a challenge, too. Little is known about his life anyway, particularly the earlier years, so I started by building a timeline which ends with the start of this book – the elusive, aforementioned 'name' and a potentially piranha-infested house.

I wrote a very carefully worded letter to 'name' asking if they wouldn't mind a chat about their possible connection with Roy James. I added the word 'possible' as a get-out clause, giving them the option of simply saying that they didn't know him so I'd leave them in peace, even though I know they did know him. I have no intention of being a Louis Theroux with this, standing around awkwardly in peoples' kitchens and asking uncomfortable questions for a cheap laugh on TV. Nor doing it like investigative reporter Roger Cook and getting punched in the chops on someone's doorstep.

Roy James was a criminal and associated with some deeply unpleasant characters at times. And some mysterious ones, like 'name', who must be about 80 years old now and was probably rather confused by my letter. Soon, I have a missed call from an unusual number and, later, an email. 'Name' doesn't remember much about Roy but is very happy to talk. 'Name', as it happens, could talk for England and confirms some things that'll come later in this book. After a very long and friendly call, they tell me, in that blunt fashion that older folks have – 'I don't think I'd want to read your book.' No problem, you can join the tens of millions of others who won't. Then, frustratingly, 'I don't want to be named in your book. Roy knew some horrible people.' I agree to this, because, frankly, he did know some horrible people and so we'll call this person 'name' from here.

In 2021, and also 2019 (we're working backwards, remember), the popular TV show The Crown was filmed at various locations, including Doneraile Street in Fulham, South West London. I say popular show, I haven't seen it. Ex-Prime Minister Sir John Major called some scenes 'a barrel-load of malicious nonsense', which sounds like it is actually probably very good. Doneraile Street, today, is a smart row of bay-fronted houses with balconies and seven-figure price tags. Google Street View shows trees in bloom and a traffic warden about to inflict some misery on a hatchback.

I don't know what scenes from The Crown were filmed there, but I do know that certain props were stolen at the time, including silverware and a replica Fabergé egg. Knowing that Roy was a silversmith, and a thief, I double-checked the dates and am fairly certain he wasn't involved on account of being dead for over 20 years. Roy was a petty criminal before he was a big one. But he was born here, in this street, when Fulham was a very different place. I will come back to Doneraile Street later/earlier/other.

Writing backwards feels like a positive way to tell a story. No unhappy endings, deaths reverse into births, sunset becomes sunrise. On the other hand, the happy return of a stolen Brabham means that we'll then have to talk about its inevitable theft beforehand.

Chapter 2 – 2018, Paraparaumu

In 2018, The New Zealand Herald reported on the recovery of a 1962 Brabham BT2. You'll find this information on their website, if you can fight off the pop-up adverts for long enough to uncover the text in the article. Using online newspapers' sites as a source of information is frustrating for two reasons; one, the damn pages are infested with adverts and two, the quality of journalism ain't what it used to be. 'The car was reportedly used as the getaway car in the Great Train Robbery by driver Roy 'The Weasel' James', says the article. You'll probably know that they actually used Land Rovers and a truck, which would make sense when shifting a huge quantity of heavy mail sacks. I cannot think of a more inappropriate vehicle to use in such an operation than a highly strung, single-seat racing car, not designed for road use, such as the Brabham. Still, they got the basics right. He once owned this car. I got RSI from clicking 'X' on all the pop-ups when learning this, then logged into Twitter to receive a message from Bobby Slowik's nephew, James Roy, who helpfully confirmed that he had never robbed a train; 'that is not me'.

Roy's Brabham has an interesting history. On importation to New Zealand, they found that some of the chassis tubes had been cut, presumably by authorities looking for hidden cash, knowing that the car carried a reputation thanks to that previous owner. There's a website which is simultaneously helpful and confusing and leads me to think that there may have been two cars with the same chassis or registration number – the recovered/stolen one in New Zealand was rebuilt from bits. Another may have the same number. Both will have been bashed and rebuilt to varying degrees, as racing cars of any era, let alone those of the lively '60s, will have seen some action.

This BT2 was recovered from a place called Lower Hutt in 2018, having been stolen from Paraparaumu Beach the year before, when it was stored inside a caravan. It's thought that the thieves didn't know what was inside when they stole the caravan and made a half-arsed attempt at dismantling the exceptionally rare car when they realised it would be nigh-on impossible to sell. In an interesting parallel, Roy had an older sister, Joanne, who moved to New Zealand probably sometime in the '80s. Unlike the car, Joanne disappeared without a trace and even friends from England have been unable to track her down. I will assume that she is no longer with us.

Back to the Brabham. John Rapley, the owner, said 'I never believed I would get a racing car like this – the car is very special to me. I built it up from a bit of wreckage – and the car has a big history.' Denny Hulme, the winner of the Formula One Championship in '67, had owned this car, probably before Roy James had it. Hulme was nicknamed 'The Bear' and liked to drive barefoot. He had the nickname on account of his gruff nature and not, to my childish disappointment, because he liked to poo in the woods.

From there, the car passed to fellow Kiwi Graham McRae, a man who raced in Formula 5000 and did a single lap in the Formula One World Championship. John Rapley, happily reunited with his car, said 'everyone remembers it from the '60s'. It's a sleek, delicate, elegant machine and I'd love a drive in one someday. We all have that one car we miss. This one must be Roy's.

Something happened in 2016/2015 that sort of buggered up the research for this book, and it's mostly my own fault. In the throes of some domestic bother, and with quite a lot on my plate, I had blagged a new, long-wheelbase Jaguar XJR from Jag's press department and convinced media giant CBS's YouTube channel, Carfection, to let me make a film about why London's baddies preferred driving Jaguars.

Together with my mate Darryl, I told the story of the Great Train Robbery and Jaguars and painted loads of 11s on local roads and flipping well loved it. I returned the car to Jaguar with the rear tyres down to the cords and the trip computer showing a tiny number next to MPG and a zero next to RANGE. I've been fortunate enough to scrounge some fabulous cars over the years for various stunts, but that XJR remains my favourite. I actually wanted to properly rob a bank or something, but my mate is a bit more sensible than me. Also, local banks are now only open for 15 minutes every third Shrove Tuesday or something, but your business is important to us, so please use our app at double-u, double-u, double-u etc. Bank robbery nowadays is best done online.

The problem with my flaky state at the time was that my research was a bit slapdash. I'm not saying it's perfect now, either, but I can two-finger type this out at my leisure, make notes and cross reference things without a cameraman tapping his watch and rolling his eyes at me. Hello Nick, if you're reading. So I said a few things about Jaguar, and Roy, that I now cannot corroborate. I said he was a vegetarian, for example, which I'm now pretty sure is bollocks. And it has caused a bit of bother elsewhere, as endless authors have since published yet more books about the Great Train Robbery and repeated the same things. Stuff I cannot find anywhere pre-2016 appeared on the film, thanks to me, and now it regularly appears in other people's books. Sorry about that.

The film went out to just under a million subscribers and I didn't get sued by anyone, so it couldn't have been that far off, could it? Fortunately for me, the broadcaster who owns the rights got sold after my little film was made and then folded. Around the same time, I believe Roy's daughter, Rachel, died in Essex of an overdose. Nothing in the news, just a digital clue on the internet and a mention from someone who knew her is my only evidence. When I gave the car back to Jaguar, they looked it over and suggested that, in the state it was in, that I buy it. I couldn't afford it, plus I knew how the car had been treated.

In 2006 or thereabouts, Roy's two daughters were given a van of his belongings that a friend had kept and approximately £20k each. This was his legacy. It didn't seem much considering his slice of the Great Train Robbery was in the region of £163k. And it seems even less when you start to unearth the other things he did, but Roy wasn't good with money. His daughters were also given his ashes, which, I am told, were sprinkled on the track at Silverstone.

Formal permission was not given for this, so Roy was surreptitiously sprinkled from a car window at speed. This seemed a little implausible to me until I was chatting with a friend who admitted to driving someone up the hill at Goodwood to similarly dispose of a loved one from the window of a Rolls-Royce. Apparently, it's a thing. If anyone is reading this, then I'd like my remains to be fly-tipped in a lay-by just to antagonise the local council.

Chapter 3 – 2004, Mansfield

And to York, England. It's 2004 and Bonhams are holding an auction. Withdrawn just before the sale, one lot is, aside from the Brabham, much of what was left of Roy's belongings. The lot included '12 silver plate trophies and cups, 2 helmets with assorted visors, tear-offs and a helmet bag, racing balaclava, a pair of racing boots, assorted newspaper cuttings magazines and 4 photographs, together with other personal effects comprising 1 prayer books, 1 bible, 3 passports and two portraits'. No amount of badgering Bonhams resulted in a response about this intriguing haul other than the lot was withdrawn in a dispute over ownership. I *thought* (use of italics there for emphasis) that it came from a Mansfield family who had hidden Roy's mate and fellow train robber, Jimmy White. Why would Londoner White want to hide in *Mansfield* (use of italics for snobbery) of all places?!

The answer may be that White had a mate there who hid him for cash. Anyway, White was described as having the ability to make himself invisible, even in Mansfield. He and Roy were cellmates at one time and they had taken up portrait painting inside. It's reasonable to assume that the two portraits of Roy listed at Bonhams were ones painted by White. I think he was one of his few friends from his time train robbing. White was skilled at picking locks and was a bit of a loner. Roy had worked as a silversmith and enjoyed the solitary nature of racing. I can see a friendship and imagine him treasuring these portraits.

When you're rich, locked up and infamous, I cannot imagine being able to form proper friendships. The rest of the Bonhams listing is similarly intriguing. I had never had him down as the religious type, so why save a prayer book and bible? Perhaps it was an heirloom from his beloved mother. Three passports?! For a man who spent a large chunk of his life in jail, that's rather unusual. Perhaps they weren't all his own passports. And why save newspaper cuttings? He seldom made the press for anything other than bad news. In the '90s, towards the end of his life, he said 'I wish I could turn the clock back. It was 30 years ago. It's not an ordinary crime where you can become a nonentity.' Well, now I'm writing a book about you, Mr Weasel.Following quite some time looking into White, I found an old girlfriend of Roy's who lived in the same area around the time of the auction. Someone I had been warned to stay away from (which I did). She'd been given some of his things for safekeeping at some point, her version of safekeeping perhaps being to stick them up for auction. Quite a few people diddled Roy over the years.

Seven years before the auction of his belongings, and around the time I was having my enjoyment of a classic film spoiled by an elderly relative, comes Roy James' death at the Royal Brompton Hospital. This hospital was originally founded as the 'Hospital for Consumption and Diseases of the Chest' and diseases of the chest is sort of what killed Roy. Today, the Royal Brompton is still a leading hospital for heart surgery and says that, thanks to medical advances in the '90s, when Roy was on the table getting sliced up, 'many patients could now avoid open-heart surgery and recover more quickly'. Well, he didn't. A triple bypass is tricky enough today but 30 years ago, it was quite a big deal. He'd had medical treatment for a dicky heart and the surgeon was looking for volunteers for a new technique. Roy volunteered, as did one other person. They made it. Roy didn't. His friends point to this as an act of selflessness on his part; probably it was, possibly he just wanted to live a bit longer.

He died in August 1997, before his 62nd birthday, and there are barely any obituaries other than the one I read, and, assuming he was conscious after anaesthetic, it must have been a painful, horrible end.

At the funeral, the media were absent and heavies lined the churchyard to maintain privacy. Peter Procter and David Brodie gave eulogies, both men I managed to track down. Train robbers attended and Francis Davidson Fraser was there, better known as Mad Frankie Fraser. I didn't track him down because (a) he's scary and (b) he's dead. A young woman who was present said 'I've never seen so many big men cry so hard.' Roy was in an open coffin, with a floral tribute spelling ROYSIE. The vicar, talking about Roysie's friendships, mentioned Ronnie Biggs – and the atmosphere went 'very, very quiet'. He couldn't have known that there was tension surrounding the relationship between these two men that went back years.

The media barely reported Roy's death, but one quoted fellow train robber Ronnie Biggs, 68, from his home in Brazil, saying 'It is very sad. I didn't know him before the robbery, but we spent time in prison together and he was great company.' He was being diplomatic. They didn't get on. This news was partially overshadowed by reports on the same day from Gary Glitter saying he'd like to do another 10 years in the music industry, although at exactly the same time he did that interview, he'd just dropped his not-very-PC PC off at PC World in Bristol. I'd heard that there had been some sort of experimental surgery done in an attempt to save Roy's life and that a friend had paid £20k for him to go private at the Brompton as he would not have lived long enough to survive the waiting list.

His last words were 'I'm going to have to surrender, I am not going to get out of this one.' And he didn't. As we're writing this story backwards, we now have life to look forward to.

Chapter 4 – '97, Marylebone

Better news for Roy, earlier in '97, was being released from jail. Had he served the full term of his original sentence for train robbing, this could have been his release date, but he'd been out earlier, and this is for another crime, post-train robbery. When earlier releases were celebrated, this one was a muted affair, as, essentially, his life was buggered. He was in very ill health with the heart condition which nobbled him a few months later and one chapter sooner than this one. He couldn't do ten stairs without stopping for breath. No amount of money would have been any help to him. He was reportedly a great father to his daughters. His ex-wife remarried. And he was alive.

The Coventry Telegraph, in what must have been a slow news day, published the story of 'The Crime of the Century'. Again. Roy must have been sick of hearing this, so many years after the event. 'You have to live with being a train robber. Whatever you do, you are a train robber', he said.

At this point in my research, I decided to work a bit harder in tracking down people in his life and wrote to the most famous name on my scruffy hit list; Bernie Ecclestone. He is a listed director of a London-based property management company which could easily be a front for some financial shenanigans or other, unless his lawyer is reading this, then it's not. I found an address for the company in Marylebone and wrote him the following letter.

Dear Mr Ecclestone,

I am researching the life of Roy James with the intention of publishing a book on his interesting life. I'm aware your paths crossed, many years ago, and wondered if you had a moment to share any anecdotes with me? My phone number is XXXXX XXXXXX. I have also enclosed a stamped addressed envelope in case you'd rather reply in writing.

Yours,

Richard von Duisberg

My phone number isn't a load of kisses, obviously, that's me obscuring it for the purposes of this book. I didn't bother with an email address as Bernie doesn't do email. I did use my real address on the return envelope and hoped that me including a stamp would appeal to his famously money-grabbing nature and/or perhaps put a smile on his wrinkly fizzog and prompt him to reply. I've used a nom de plume for years because I have a semi-sensible day job that isn't really compatible with writing what my least favourite daughter describes as 'books that your mates probably read on the toilet'. It's also helpful when writing a book about someone who, in later years, regaled friends with advice on how to bury a body. You bury them standing up; apparently, it makes them harder to spot from the air. At the end of his life, Roy was very short of money and was doing some dangerous things with scary people.

Chapter 5 – '96, Kawasaki

I believe Roy had been ill in jail, in '96. From a legal standpoint, a quick google says that you cannot slander the dead. So I could say 'Roy had been ill in jail, in 1996' without 'I believe' preceding it and the fear of getting sued by anyone. But I only want to write the facts as I find them, unless another writer is reading this to write yet another book about the Great Train Robbery, in which case Roy was also a keen Morris dancer with incurable dandruff. In the same year, '96, his ex-wife Anthea married a chap called Philip in Surrey.

I spent some time investigating Phil before coming to the conclusion that, even if I could find him, I wouldn't know what to ask him. There's no public interest in this and, later, I was told that Roy thought Phil was an OK sort of chap. I came to the same conclusion about Anthea and Roy's daughters. I'd worry that they'd think I was somehow trying to glamorise the life of a man who did so much harm, or conversely paint him as Satan, although at this point of my research, I wasn't convinced I knew who he was yet, despite a ton of notes and many leads to follow.

By now, Roy was broke and contemplating some seriously hare-brained schemes. Kawasaki made the ZXi 900cc Jet Ski from 1995 to 1997. The timeline of this fact doesn't square perfectly with this next anecdote about Roy's life, but I was told a lengthy story by his friend, David Brodie, in Brodie's kitchen, which I'll recount here in an appropriate font.

Roy said he wanted to buy this new ZXi Jet Ski as it was the most powerful one available and, with a modified, long-range fuel tank and a waterproof compartment, would be suitable for drug smuggling. It would do 50 knots. Roy said he intended to jet-ski from East Anglia to the Continent, collect a load of drugs and jet-ski back, all under the cover of darkness. Roy reckoned he could do this return trip in under three hours.

Comic Sans, a firm favourite of school noticeboards and Facebook Karens. The chances of doing this jet-ski trip, undetected and not being battered to death by waves and passing ships, in the same time it takes my missus to decide which hat to wear, seems impossible to me. I also had to politely question how well David Brodie knew Roy, until Brodie produced photographs of them together and, standing awkwardly in his kitchen, I felt exactly like Louis Theroux, which is something I'd promised to try and avoid. The dates can't be right; the jet-ski production didn't align with Roy's timeline, but what about the journey?

I then recalled, from distant memory, the conviction of a young roofer called Dale McLaughlan. During COVID-19 lockdown, in the middle of winter, the love-struck McLaughlan rode a jet ski from Scotland to the Isle of Man as he was missing his girlfriend. A 25-mile journey he expected to take 40 minutes took over four hours. If Roy took the shortest crossing of the English Channel on his jet ski at the same pace as a horny Scotsman, and immediately returned, it would have taken him eight hours. And that's assuming he could find the drug smugglers at the other end and load immediately, in the dark.

Roy never attempted the trip, but the fact that I'd spent some time calculating the viability of it means that either I subconsciously think he might have been capable of it or I'm pretty poor at basic time/distance calculations. McLaughlan, who couldn't even swim and had never ridden a jet ski before, by the way, got three days in jail and was banned from the Isle of Man for life. The girlfriend dumped him and was later convicted of being drunk and disorderly and spitting at a policeman. Ahhh, young love.

Chapter 6 – '95, Davy Crockett

Another scheme Roy supposedly investigated at this time, according to his friend Brodie, who was kindly filling me with coffee and ignoring his hyperactive dog, was that of, hang on, font time, **turning a car factory into a marijuana factory.** Roy would have had little or no money to invest, and his health was poor, but a man supposedly turned up and measured the unit and estimated costs for shutter doors, a new internal wall and a large chimney. Coincidentally, this actually happened many years later at another motoring industry business.

The Pilgrim Cars company in Sussex had an owner called Den Tanner who covered his factory roof in solar panels to help create sufficient energy to not only power his modest kit-car business making replicas of the famous AC Cobra, but to power the lighting and heating needed to grow industrial amounts of marijuana. Den was an obnoxious character (source reference; my own experience) who denied being involved in the drugs trade, before being sent to jail for 3 years. He was also fined c.£220k for this, 18% of which was awarded to the police.

This weirdly means that Sussex Police are, essentially, drug-financed. Tanner discovered God on his release, Roy never built his marijuana factory and the site owner laughed the idea off. Oh, and in Fulham, a depressed 'Lucky Terry' Hogan, who had also been known as Harry Booth, jumped to his death.

These were Roy's final years and he had just £6,800 left, said Brodie, who was so busy chatting that I did not get a chance to ask why there was a bottle of unusual cider and a book called 'Teach Your Dog Welsh' on his table. Roy had just been released from Leicester's Gartree prison and told stories of mixing with the Krays inside. After having checked that they're both properly dead and, therefore, unlikely to get me, I can say I've never understood the fascination with the Krays. Roy said that 'Reggie was alright, but', in a no-shit-Sherlock moment of character analysis, 'Ronnie was dangerous.'

Prison kept Roy fit and warders arranged a race around the prison between Roy and a boxer called Paul Sykes. Sykes has been called 'one of the most difficult prisoners in the country' and even his photograph is scary. He looks brutal. He was 6'3" tall, almost a foot taller than Roy, and a fitness fanatic who held records for weightlifting. The race involved various push-ups, lifts and sprints and was won, to some applause, by Roy. Sykes was an extremely violent man, he's dead now, and I think both of his sons are currently serving life sentences for murder. Wisely, Roy avoided Sykes inside, especially after this race. Sykes once made a Davy Crockett hat out of the prison cat.

Chapter 7 – '94, AK-47

February 1994 sees Roy in the dock for the second biggest crime he was convicted of. He claimed to have had a 'thunderstorm in the mind' but was sent down for 6 years. He only served three, due in part to the heart disease which was starting to bother him. His crime, committed in '93, was that of shooting his ex-father-in-law and beating his ex-wife with a revolver, in front of their children. When I started working on this book, and weighed up what kind of person he might be, I wondered what had happened in his life to shape him. Racing is an expensive business. Stealing used bank notes could, at a stretch, be passed off as a victimless crime of sorts. I wondered if I was starting to identify with Roy as a fellow maverick. I once went a whole month with an accidentally lapsed MOT, and rarely tip more than a few pounds in restaurants, for example. Well, unless the service is exceptional. And the train driver who got walloped, well, the robbers and their legal people long clung to the notion that he died of causes unrelated to the attack.

So I had this rough image of a working-class Londoner trying to break into racing and eventually committing crime to fund it. A kind of motoring Robin Hood, if you will. The reports of the attack in '93 dispel such ideas even quicker than Bernie's secretary bins unsolicited letters. There was a quote from one of his daughters (depending on which one, she would have been approximately 5 or 8 years old at the time) begging him to put the gun down. He was usually a doting father but it's a horrible image. In court, having hired a rather expensive defence lawyer, he said he had 'flipped his lid'. He was trying to claim temporary insanity as his defence, which the judge dismissed, rightly so, as rubbish.

But I think there's remorse when he was interviewed by a newspaper and said 'I wish I had the courage to blow my own brains out.' Brodie said he took ownership of Roy's assets, sold his house and paid off his debts. He was, undoubtedly, a very good friend to Roy when he was short of friends. After clearing his debts, Roy was left with a paltry £76k, which Brodie says he put into a bank on the Isle of Man.

Roy entertained a few close friends here, riding on quad bikes around the grounds and rode his powerful Kawasaki – 'his legs barely reached the ground' said a friend. He went to the shops in a pickup truck and stayed off the radar. He loved animals and had a huge Rottweiler called Merlin to deter unwanted visitors. Roy preferred to visit others, instead of them coming to him.

I recall a flight back to the UK from somewhere in Eastern Europe some years ago. An excited young couple in front of me were watching the map screen as we approached London, chatting in a language I didn't speak; 'To jest takie podniecające. Spójrz tam w dół. *Surrey*. Co mówi mapa? *Surrey*... AONB. Co to jest Surrey AONB? *Area Of Natural Beauty!*' said the lad. 'Nie' laughed his girlfriend 'nie tylko Natural Beauty... *OUTSTANDING* Natural Beauty!' I laughed too; there was just enough English in the sentence for me to work out they were laughing at the snobbery of an area described as not just 'natural beauty', but '*outstanding* natural beauty'. Ah well, you had to be there. But it sums up the 'leafy Surrey hills' home-counties vibe of the area.

In '93, Roy was living here, in a place called Headley, behind gates and fences, with ponies in the field. He was rarely seen locally. The place looks the same today and is worth millions, owned by investment banking horsey types who'd probably be as appalled if they knew a criminal once lived there as they would at Polish people turning up to look at their *outstanding* natural beauty. In this house, Roy had full-time care of his two daughters and his ex-wife, Anthea, was returning the children to him on what was an access day. She was at the house together with her father, David Wadlow, who was a bank inspector working for NatWest, not Robert Wadlow, who was the world's tallest man, which caused me some excitement when my research got a bit confused after a few beers one evening. Let's have another paragraph; this is an important part of the story.

Roy had agreed a financial settlement with Anthea of £150k, to be paid within a certain timeframe. He had wanted to remortgage the house for half a million. One single report (the Leatherhead Advertiser, if you'd care to check) mentioned that the money was needed to help fund a legal claim against an ex-girlfriend. Roy was insistent at talking to David, his father-in-law, who, in turn, didn't want to talk to him.

As the children were being unloaded from the car, to return to their home with Roy, he lost his temper, took a gun and shot David three times. At first, said David, he thought it was just a starting pistol as it was a little gun. Two shots went through his shoulder and the initial lack of pain confused him, but the third shot could have killed him. There was chaos. His daughter was begging him to put down the gun. I can only imagine Anthea screaming. Roy hit her repeatedly with his pistol. He refused to call an ambulance, before (he says, anyway) he called the police himself. Later, a police officer received an award for helping to disarm him. Why would he need to be disarmed if he called the police himself, as he claimed?

Snippets of info like this help to build a clearer image of who Roy was. It's a horrible moment and his 6-year sentence seems light to me, and is perhaps a reflection that, although it had been many years since the train robbery, and his other crimes, he was still a man wealthy enough to afford legal representation of a very high quality. Roy said he had gotten the gun from his friend, ex-train robber Bobby Welch. Roy said that he'd taken it from Bobby as he was worried about Bobby's suicidal state after a bodged leg operation, whereas on another date, Bobby claimed that Roy had actually provided him with a gun. Bobby died in 2023, by the way, the last of the Great Train Robbery gang to go.

Perhaps this incident was the culmination of what must have been a very tense time for all involved. One has to ask why Roy needed the money so badly. Funding a legal claim? We'll come to the other women as we go back to his earlier life, but there were too few 'steady' ones. There was mention of a doctor he was dating, a relationship that went sour years before.

I wonder if, at this point, as he'd totally given up on motorsport, he was hooked on money. If all that mattered was money. If money drove him so crazy that he'd shoot people. David later lived in a nice apartment in East London and didn't publicly speak of the incident. Roy, as we know, went inside again. After reconstructing this scene from contemporary reports and having sifted through a digital skipfull of online rubbish, I was quite happy that I'd got this important chapter in Roy's life correct with all facts covered. And then, in writing, I find a snippet which says that Roy had hidden an AK-47 inside a plastic tube in a specific location in the grounds of the Surrey house. The same house which now has Rupert and Tabitha double-barrelled-nanny-says-the-Tesla-needs-charging-before-pony-club living there. I do not know what to do with this information.

I looked at the house on Google Maps and figured I could climb over a fence and poke about myself with a metal detector at the spot described. If he were alive, the Weasel himself might do something like this. Then I decided to write a letter to the homeowner instead, explaining there might be some nefarious treasure on their property. But what if the person living there now knows this already or is some Freddy the frenulum-snapper gangster type? Perhaps the owner would just report it to the police and my daft penname wouldn't be enough to hide from overly inquisitive rozzers who would switch off their bodycams and wallop me into revealing my sources. Do they do that? I think I've read too many gangster books lately. This information is probably more trouble than it's worth, so let's say it's all made up and move on.

Chapter 8 – '92, Purple urn

Approximately a year before the shooting, Roy's mother, Violet, died. She was 80 years old. I had wondered if the prayer book and bible that appeared at Bonhams were from her, gifts to help her son find the right path in life when he was in one of the many jails that housed him over the years. He mentioned the upset of her death and their close relationship in his defence for the shooting. But, no, she wasn't a particularly religious woman. Violet had visited him inside and was perhaps the only constant in his life. Roy had other family members, but she was the most important.

I paid for a subscription to Ancestry.com to rifle through Roy's family tree. The adverts on TV for this, and similar websites, are overly slick and cheesy. Grainy film footage of handsome, mustachioed gentlemen, sepia photographs of elegant ladies in bonnets and voiceover gushing 'My ancestor was a beautiful Italian princess!' My arse was she. The lightest shake of any family tree will see leaves drop bearing the cold, hard fact that your ancestor probably died young of some horrible disease after working down some miserable Midlands coalmine.

Roy described to a friend how his mother had what we now know to be dementia. She was accusing neighbours of stealing from her and, eventually, she accused Roy of stealing from her, too. From his letters, we know he worried about her. He was worried about her drinking, saying 'she starts fights'. She didn't like using the telephone, so would miss trains and other appointments. He kept her ashes in a purple urn on his mantelpiece. No illicit scatterings for her.

Her relatively long life, and the fact that his father lived to be 71 (we'll get to him in a bit), don't point to any congenital heart disease issues. But Roy was already getting out of shape. He led an undeniably stressful life, it has to be said, and he did not drink or smoke, but he did like fast food. I asked Brodie if Roy was a vegetarian, as I'd seen that on YouTube somewhere in a documentary about Jaguars, and he looked at me like it was the most stupid thing he'd ever heard. So that's a 100% confirmed no, then.

Roy and Anthea were divorced in '91. I don't know what she was thinking marrying a man whose nickname was the Weasel. In Greek culture, a weasel is supposed to bring bad luck, especially to households where a girl is about to be married. Legend says an unhappy bride was transformed into a weasel who delights in destroying wedding dresses. Respecting her privacy means we only have his side of the story. He said she was an alcoholic and he was worried about her driving with their children in the car. She'd checked in, and prematurely out, of a rehabilitation clinic. And he mentioned psychiatric problems.

He'd bought her an expensive Mercedes-Benz, paid for the ponies in the field, and the field, and financed some cosmetic surgery, so he said. There was a considerable age gap and she'd taunted him about this, saying things like 'you smell like my granddad'. My granddad probably smelled like a coal miner and lived in Leicester. Thanks, Ancestry.com.

Roy was always smartly turned out. At one time, a tailor bravely chased him for unpaid debts and uncollected suits when he was on the run. During divorce proceedings, Roy said he was spending £8,800 a year on school fees (and this is in 1991, remember!). I got the feeling he was bitter about money and the difference in lifestyle and expectations. Anthea had nagged him, saying 'your teeth are going yellow' and 'what will you look like in another ten years?' Well, he'd look dead, as it turned out.

My description of Roy thus far is a bit of a photofit. I'm working off other people's descriptions, media reports, snippets from the papers, bilge off the internet and guesswork. Those who met him might have their own take on his personality, or lifestyle, which I have to factor in when trying to find out who the 'real' Weasel was. I described this problem to Mia Forbes Pirie, daughter of Val Pirie, who appears earlier in Roy's life (and, therefore, mostly later in this book). From her own website Mia is 'an international mediator, facilitator and coach'. Brodie, who we met earlier, enjoyed telling some tall stories and Procter, who we'll meet in about a hundred pages' time, was very keen on facts and dates and details. Others I've dealt with might have had an axe to grind with Roy or insisted on anonymity, which I respect. Mia Forbes Pirie's professional skills ('I'm a recovering lawyer') meant that I didn't have to pick my words quite so carefully when asking about her relationship with Roy, who she warmly described as a father figure. Trying to show off with what I thought was a clever opening question, I asked her which famous person should play Roy in a film of his life. 'The little one from The Two Ronnies', she said, before asking me if I'd seen the film Crash, 'but not the sex version.'

Mia explained that, along with Stirling Moss (her mum's old boss) and Peter Janson, Roy had been a father figure to her as a child when she was living in a flat in Westminster. Roy visited Val when she was pregnant (which must have been soon after he was released) and continued to visit when Mia was a child. He'd bring crayons and toys and play patiently with her, always smiling, always happy and with a twinkle in his eye. Mia pointed out how harsh Roy's sentence had been, although admitted she struggled to put into context the shooting of his father-in-law. She explained to me that everyone has a scale of one to ten, where her ten might be shouting at her husband, Roy's was apparently shooting someone. He had, she said, 'amazing charisma'. To sort of benchmark what amazing charisma looks like to Mia, in case that means people like Ronnie Corbett, I looked into the other father figures in her life.

Mia's mum worked for Stirling Moss, published a book about him and even the most sheltered of people will know who he is. He was once stopped for speeding in the Mersey Tunnels and asked by a copper 'who do you think you are, Stirling Moss?' His answer in the affirmative didn't get him off the fine. Indeed a charismatic chap. And to check Mia's take on Roy's 'amazing charisma', I had a google of Peter Janson and was delighted to find that he was an absolute bloody charmer. He was a bearded Kiwi racer who lived a playboy lifestyle, owned an elephant and once changed his name by deed poll to NGK Sparkplugs in order to circumvent a ban on logos on his car. Visitors to his house included Sherpa Tenzing Norgay and Olivia Newton-John. He entertained them wearing a brocaded, red velvet smoking jacket. To keep his sponsor, Cadburys, happy, he once stopped his car during a race to throw chocolate bars into the crowd. He'd park where he liked and just pay the fine, confidence coming from having been a captain in the army in India. Now *that's* charisma.

For Roy to fit into the same bracket as these characters shows that he was a hell of a man. Mia said that, on a visit to her house once, she tried to explain the awkward lock on the toilet door – Roy told her 'don't worry, I can work it out, I'm a burglar'. She said that he couldn't help himself and that, in some respects, it's a healthy lifestyle. It was certainly an exciting one. Mia talked of victimless crimes and the East End code of not hurting women or children, and was polite enough not to chew my ear off when I asked if that might be a bit of a cliché pedalled by gangsters. In Roy's case, it's not, she said. Mia signed off by suggesting I read 'Hillbilly Elegy', which is something about socioeconomic problems in Ohio and sounds nowhere near as interesting as her words on Roy, Stirling Moss and Mr NGK Sparkplugs.

Chapter 9 – '90, Porky and Scarface

In his later years, Roy had lived a mostly private life. He'd given up on his dreams of racing and had only a little contact with the motorsport crowd. He'd tried to settle down and bring up a family, away from the limelight. Some of the other robbers had courted the media, people like Ronnie Biggs. In reality, Ronnie was a minor figure in the gang, but noisily mixed with rock and rollers, footballers and other attention-seekers, happy to talk to anyone. You can read this in any one of dozens of books.

Some of the train robbers tried to fade away. Roy said, in the '90s, that he took no pride in the robbery. But he did occasionally cross paths with his former train robbers. In May 1990, with what looks like his wife, Anthea, he attended the funeral of Charlie Wilson. Roy had argued with press photographers attending the funeral at Streatham Cemetery in South London. A gathering of black-clad gangsters like this made for a great photo opportunity and, no doubt, photographers from the red tops goaded them to get a reaction, and a story. This tactic might work with 'slebs, but you'd be brave poking any of the black-suited, raw-knuckled crowd at Charlie Wilson's funeral.

Charlie had been shot dead on his doorstep at his home in Marbella, Spain, in a matter related to a drugs feud. The attack was carried out by men nicknamed Porky and Scarface. The man who had ordered the hit was later killed, Scarface was shot in the spine and Porky went on the run. What is it with London gangsters and nicknames? Roy himself, as we know, had carried the sobriquet 'The Weasel'. It is assumed that the name stuck because of his slight, lithe build and history of burglary. But even that's not what it seems.

My research was now starting to unearth people, like 'name', Brodie and others. People who were willing to talk about Roy, not just people who had an opinion on the Great Train Robbery or who were keen to tell me about Bernie Ecclestone. There was a pattern emerging of those who knew him from racing who (mostly, but not completely) thought he was humble, sincere, keen to learn and happy to fit in. And conversely, in his personal life (family aside), people who were, frankly, rather scared of him. This might have been due to his criminal associations.

At this point, the only incidence of violence he'd committed was the one which happened in a Surrey AONBWAGUTP (Area of Outstanding Natural Beauty With A Gun Under The Paddock). Putting that aside, the only report I had heard from the racing community about him being in any way unpleasant was from someone who spotted him overtaking 'discourteously, in Suffolk' when driving home after a race. Those people didn't know Roy as the Weasel. They knew him as a racing driver.

In '88, when he was still married, his wife Anthea gave birth to a daughter, Samantha. And in '85, they had Rachel. I had one last, delicate attempt to contact Samantha, still unsure how they'd react to some clumsy amateur trying to write a book about their notorious father.

I eventually found who I was quite sure was her, the date of birth matching, a name which tallied, she even has the same eyes in a picture online. She had a webpage advertising fitness classes and a mobile number was listed. Very carefully, I composed a text message. 'Hello. Sorry to disturb you. I'm a writer, currently researching for a book on Roy James (born in London in 1935, died 1997). Might you be related? If you had a moment to respond I'd appreciate it. Thanks. Richard Duisberg.' A day or two later, a reply pinged. 'Hi. I don't think so. I asked my parents and they don't think so either.' If she'd asked her father, and he wasn't dead, and she wasn't a medium, then he couldn't be Roy. I was amused and relieved and thanked her anyway.

Brodie then gave me a phone number for Samantha, which I texted and got a reply of 'no, that's not me'. I then learn that he'd only spoken to her once since Roy's ashes were scattered almost 20 years ago, so maybe the number was wrong or had changed or something. Brodie told an outrageous story about Roy and cut-price prostitutes, and I asked him how Roy's daughter might feel if she read it. 'Oh, she'd find it funny', he said. 'She's a chip off the ol' block.' I'm not inclined to find out. Besides, I had a lead on another facet of Roy's life that I needed to investigate. So, hands up – who likes recruitment consultants? No, me neither.

Chapter 10 – '80s, Saudis

There are two people with the name Charles Crichton-Stuart here. One appears to be a recruitment consultant who, according to LinkedIn, studied law and is not dead, so I'll tread carefully before being rude about him or associating him with a scam involving Roy and gullible Saudi royals. There's another one, quite possibly related, who died in the Philippines when on a trip hunting for sunken treasure. Did people like Roy ever have normal friends? A Steve who works for Wickes and fits bathrooms for cash at weekends, perhaps? Or a Claire who posts 'to whoever parks their van outside my house' on Facebook? No, it seems not.

The Charles Crichton-Stuart here is the dead one, once part of the Haas Lola Formula One team and was somehow involved in the Williams Formula One sponsorship deal with Saudia, the flag carrier of Saudi Arabia. His cousin was Johnny Dumfries, who Crichton-Stuart found a job for at Williams driving the van. Dumfries was the 7th Marquess of Bute, heir to a large fortune and went on to be a handy racer at the highest levels. Interesting family.

Anyway, in the '80s, our Crichton-Stuart was working as a schmoozer of some sort in London's Clermont Club, frequented by wealthy Arabs and their groupies. Roy had some diamonds mounted on platinum rings and intended to sell them, via an enthusiastic Crichton-Stuart, to gullible Saudis trying to impress girls. Now there is nothing illegal in this that I can see, but the suspicion is that the stones were stolen.

At least two of these rings ended up being swapped for motorbikes instead, Saudis not being as gullible as expected. Roy was working in the jewellery trade in Hatton Garden, where buying, selling and quickly offloading anything iffy was the norm. Homework led me to learn that Roy had a shop there for some years. It stood on the corner of Greville Street and Hatton Garden. This address was important in Roy's life, and I had the need to somehow connect with a location. The 'Bernie's trophy' story emanates from roughly this time, and certainly this address, so a visit was in order.

Chapter 11 – '80s, Luton Airport Parkway

As I have mentioned previously, there are plenty of books on the Great Train Robbery and I feel no need to repeat much of the story here, but here comes a train story. I like a train ride but the East Midlands Railway service from Leicester to London is expensive and packed. The only amusement to be had is standing in the busy corridor with one foot in each carriage, either side of the concertina cover thing that connects carriages, 'surfing' along sideways. Acting a bit mental is a great way to get some space to yourself on a packed commuter train. I wanted a tiny taste of the life of crime, a soupçon of the train robbery lifestyle, so bought a cup of tea and paid not using my own bank card but with the joint account bank card the missus says I am only allowed to use for groceries. Man, it feels good to be such a dangerous maverick. I hold eye contact with a fellow commuter for slightly too long. I am not to be messed with. Rattling through Market Harborough, I feel alive. By Kettering, I have tasted karma as my surf technique resulted in spilling enough tea on my trousers to be kindly offered a tissue by the passenger who I then felt guilty for staring at a bit earlier. The train then passes the scene of the greatest train robbery of all, and it's not Bridego Bridge. The greatest train robbery of all is the Luton DART.

DART stands for Direct Air-Rail Transit and describes the connection between the Midland Main Line and the worst airport in the civilised world. This connection costs, at the time of writing, £4.90 one way. The distance is 1.29 miles. This must be, in £/mile, the most expensive train journey in the world. £3.79 per mile, when you've already arrived by train at what they call Luton Airport Parkway.

Parkway is an old English word describing a desolate concrete outpost. I've not checked that, but I'm sure it's true based on visits to East Midlands Parkway, Warwick Parkway and Luton sodding Airport Parkway. The price per mile for the DART, someone at the Guardian newspaper once said, is 100 times that of an EasyJet flight to Spain. I drove to Luton airport once, but the car park caught fire. As we haul into London St Pancras, please take all your belongings with you, I repaid the joint account for my stolen tea with £2.75 from my own account and texted an explanation for my financial misdemeanour to the missus. I'm not cut out to be a gangster.

A tube to Farringdon and up for air, then Hatton Garden. Roy's two daughters, Rachel born in '85-ish and Samantha around '88, had a dad who was, officially at least, a silversmith and jeweller. This (and Soho) was his patch when he had his young family and represents a time in his life when he was trying to go straight. But there are some iffy businesses here.

My walk to Roy's old shop takes me past number 12, Hatton Garden, which was the location for Mike Reid's bent jeweller in the film, Snatch. Today, it's called Premier House and home to a IS & Co., a diamond buyer whose slogan is 'get paid for your jewellery'. As opposed to what, IS & Co., *donating* it?! Also here is Eric Ross and a Google review for their business that, edited down, says: 'I come to find out that they had switched out my centre stone and replaced it with a smaller stone [without telling me]'.

There are plenty of good reviews, too, including one from a Reshma Parbat, who says 'I wouldn't go anywhere else' and is, therefore, presumably still inside. I arrive at the location which was described as being on the corner of Hatton Garden and Greville Street. I envisaged a solitary shop with a welcoming owner who could regale me with tales of Roy working here, precisely working rare metals, honing precious stones and creating things of beauty. But I am confused. There is not one jewellers here but four, one on each corner of the crossroads.

I ordered a coffee and sat and watched. Here, people buy and sell beneath the office blocks and busy streets of London. I imagined Roy and his young assistant, Anthea (later his wife), as contestants in the car-crash classic TV show, The Apprentice. I'm sipping dishwater in Costa and mentally narrating the scene: *In this weeks' episode, which is the same as every single episode ever, the contestants are tasked with buying something on the cheap, then attempt to sell it at a wildly unrealistic price to disinterested members of the public, in between bouts of frantically shouting into a mobile and bitching. None of them will ever achieve anything meaningful in their lives.* All this set to drone footage of Central London, cut with shots of power suits, Rolls-Royces and private jets.

Actually, they made quite a good team, Roy and Anthea. She handed out leaflets in the street, he appraised the items the public might sell and they made it work. And, as a bonus, they didn't have to pretend they're sat in a boardroom instead of facing barrow boy Sugar on a TV set in West Acton, nor have Karen Brady looking at them like they were all dog dirts. Surely a *real* apprentice show would have proper apprenticeship experiences, such as low-to-medium risk horseplay, degrading initiation ceremonies and being forced to use a humiliating nickname based on the German equivalent of Wolverhampton, which you eventually grow to accept and use as a nom de plume when you publish this book.

It seems that, although Roy's business was superficially successful, he still had what a friend called 'the devil in him'. This next crime was supposedly committed during his time working in Hatton Garden, in the shop, and was done more for the adventure than the proceeds. This, like many other stunts attributed to him, was not widely reported in the press at the time and he was never convicted or even arrested in association with it. There comes a certain burden to find the truth when investigating these rumours and, while this one isn't at the 'jet-ski the Channel' level of fantasy, in comparison, it's perhaps a 'pedalo the Thames' level. For clarity, he didn't pedalo anything – he blew his neighbours' safe up.

The businesses in this area today are exceptionally aware of the importance of security and, in the late '80s, they were no different. Roy will have had a good security system for his business because (a) it was his business and (b) he was a thief and knew what thieves did. The safes of these jewellery businesses were often in the basement, which, of course, could only be accessed from the floor above. So the floor above, usually the ground floor of the building, was alarmed, bolted, covered by cameras and generally very secure.

Roy had noticed that a nearby business had a grille on the floor at the back of the building, perhaps to provide air and light to a basement beneath. A rudimentary inspection confirmed that, by removing this metal grille, little more than a flap, access could be gained to the basement below, completely bypassing the security on the ground floor. Access was one thing, but opening the safe was a different skill set, and one that Roy did not have. Underworld connections provided him with an old man who knew how to blow open a safe. It's important to note that, although the primary security technology advanced over the years, many businesses still used older safes as they were already in place and, frankly, a bit of a bugger to remove. The internet was being invented around the time of this crime, so Roy didn't have the power of Google, which, today, is full of handy guides on how to crack a safe. Roy had to rely on this old crook who took an old-fashioned approach.

Safes were generally made from cast iron. Iron is very strong, but is not impossible to break. Iron can be heated up to encourage it to become brittle, then heaved out of an upper-floor window, causing it to break open on impact. This would not work for Roy as the safe was large, exceptionally heavy and down a narrow corridor, which is connected to the upper, alarmed, floors. Also, the risk here is that, by heating the safe, you cook the contents. Fine if it's precious stones, less good if it's cash. Roy expected that there were stones in this old-fashioned safe.

A similarly brutal but sometimes effective method is to blow the lock open. The mining industry used to use lots of Polar Ammon gelignite and Polar Ajax. Either would do, but gelignite is extremely sensitive to moisture. A small amount of gelignite is then placed in a condom (you at the back, stop sniggering!) and gently poked through the lock hole in the door with a lolly stick. The open end of the condom is held in place on the outside of the door with Plasticine. Then a larger dollop of gelignite is placed on the outside of the door covering the lock mechanism area. Attaching two wires, as Roy did with his safe-breaker cowering a distance away, to the gelignite, Roy then curled up and prepared to apply the two wires to a small battery to complete a circuit and blow the door mechanism. Some doors are fitted with glass bolts which shatter on any kind of impact, springing larger, steel bolts in the door. Some require a thermic lance to cut open, but care needs to be taken so as not to nuke the goodies inside. Anyway, they caused a colossal explosion that brought part of the roof down and filled the room with plaster and dust and splinters, but the safe didn't open.

Roy and his man scarpered up through the grille, laughing. He caused lasting damage to his hearing doing this. I SAID HE CAUSED LASTING DAMAGE TO HIS HEARING. But he had enjoyed himself and didn't get nicked. I think there were different phases of his life as a criminal; this happened because he enjoyed the planning, enjoyed using the skills needed and missed the excitement of crime. I SAID HE ENJOYED... oh, forget it.

Chapter 12 – '80s, West African coastguard

Roy liked sport. Solitary sports suited his personality, and he had quite taken to sailing for a while. David Brodie told me a story that Roy had told him about stealing a boat and sailing it to the Azores. On his own. I do not know the reason for this, and it's the kind of trip that even the most seasoned of sailors would take very seriously, even with the most modern of equipment and all the safety gubbins, let alone a trimaran stolen from a boatyard in Hamble-le-Rice. Roy said he encountered, hang on... **Roy said he encountered the 'West African coast guard', who were using an oil tanker to chase smugglers as, unladen, oil tankers are extremely fast. He then ended up in Gibraltar, before dumping the boat back where he stole it from in Hampshire, and returning to London.** I have no idea of the aim of this caper, be it smuggling, drugs or perhaps the whole thing was just made up.

Brodie tells some utterly outrageous stories in general, and I could not square what I knew of Roy with the world of sailing. He supposedly owned a beautiful, teak-decked powerboat on the Med, said Brodie. My questioning of this possibly iffy anecdote cost me £220. Brodie pulled out a huge tome, his unedited, self-published memoirs and proved it. He flicked to the back and there, in black and white, is a photograph of Roy at the helm of this beautiful powerboat. Shirtless, smiling and enjoying the south of France.

Brodie said I could buy his book (there are five tomes, covering his life as a businessman and racing driver) and he'd sign it. It should be £250 but I could have it for £220, he said, as I was writing about his old mate. And Brodie is very, very funny. My rationale was that, if 10% of what he said about racing in general was true, then it would be a goldmine of information from an era I enjoy reading about. Plus I'd have evidence of Roy that helped me build the picture of his life in his later years. Maybe it would give me further insight into a fascinating era in motorsport?

After having paid, I flipped open a page at random to see a chapter called 'Wheels and tits'. This sort of unleashed a torrent of anecdotes, opinions and emotions often about some quite famous people that, even though I could quote his expensive book to cover my arse, I am not going to repeat here. As a side note, reader, I've just taken a break from writing and randomly delved into Brodie's book. He's quite a storyteller; he claims he saw Lord Lucan at Silverstone in 2001. I really, really want to believe this!

Roy had netted quite a sum of money from the train robbery, no spoiler in telling you that at this point, but in the '80s, he was back stealing from trains as he found it so easy. He would dress as a hiker in boots, woolly hat and massive rucksack and wander the marshalling yards looking for the post carriages which carried high-value mailbags. This, essentially, was the same sort of crime as the Great Train Robbery; spotting the valuable sacks, clocking which train it is on and then holding it up. But Roy knew he could steal smaller sums and conceal the crime.

He would hide in unlocked carriages, wait for mail workers to load the carriage and then ride the long train journey with the sacks, picking through the packages. At the destination, he'd hide again until the train was unloaded, sneak out of the yard and hitchhike back to London. He'd occasionally be found and would act like a lost walker, and, in one case, a sympathetic rail worker actually found him accommodation for the night and a warm meal. This for the man who had stolen the equivalent of £60 million in a similar scenario. This wasn't a particularly exciting crime and the pickings were mixed.

Eventually, he stopped doing this as the slog back to London with a heavy rucksack, at night, often in poor weather, became too much like hard work. There are so many little stories like this I was uncovering that I found it hard to assemble them in a timeline. Some overlap. Some allegedly happened when I know he was in prison. Others are so nonsensical that I've excluded them. People (some named, some not) seemed to enjoy sharing these snippets.

Getting multiple versions of the same story helped to find a 'middle path' of plausibility. Getting one-off information, unverified, made me very cautious including it. Some stories were, frankly, splendid tales but actually happened to someone else altogether. Railways seemed to form a 'target' for Roy, and the stories.

One tale, which is in writing somewhere, tells how, as a very young child, Roy told someone he would rob a big train someday. I can barely remember my own name most days. How the dickens can some befuddled pensioner remember Roy said these exact words from almost a century ago is incredible. Who knows. Roy's shop years should have been the happy ending for all this; family life and normality. But he couldn't leave the trains and adventure alone, it seems.

Chapter 13 – '83, The Hackney Rock

We are now in the early '80s, in Green Park, London. No expensive books needed to check nor reliance on flaky third-hand stories heard in a boozer; there is photographic evidence. Roy is standing beside a Jaguar Mark 2, and a Mini van, selling jewellery. The jewellery is his own and comes from a time before he had the shop, when he was working from home on Highfield Road, Purley. He's smiling, sort of, but he must be utterly fed up with the media following him around. Shutterstock wants £159 for this image and I'm a bit broke thanks to buying Brodie's books, so I'll describe it to you instead. Roy is in a sweater over a striped shirt, hands in back pockets, pen on a string around his neck, talking to a well-dressed lady who is looking at some bracelets of a sort I know Roy made, on a table. In a second picture, in the same location at the same time, he's smiling slightly sheepishly. There's a Shutterstock watermark all over everything.

Roy had a company at this time called Illuminate Ltd., which I think was to manage his jewellery business. There is nothing suspicious about this picture. An ordinary sort of man, selling nice things from a table, at the roadside of a green in London. He'd be in his late forties here. He is going straight. Actually, he *is* straight, here. It's the time of life when many blokes make a hash of their lives, buy an inappropriate sports car, drink too much and jack in a sensible job to write books. Ahem. But Roy looks happy and healthy here. I don't understand why he'd need to chase the later adventures of Hatton Garden. It's not the first time in his life where he was in a relatively comfortable position and threw it away chasing adventure. I think I need to stop putting myself in his shoes – I'd quit while I was ahead, but Roy was made differently to me. He was made differently to anyone I've met or read about.

He went to Tenerife and met a Cockney boxer called John Gardner. Roy tended to take short-term leases on properties and it's not known if this was a holiday trip or if he lived there for a while. Many gangsters would run to the sun. Known as the 'Hackney Rock', Gardner was a serious contender at one time before getting mixed up with hoodlums and moving to Newcastle. I think Gardner was in Tenerife avoiding trouble. He had fought Roy's cat in the cat hat, Paul Sykes, in '79, with Sykes going to jail 2 years later for taking out a hit on a union official in Blackpool.

Gardner had just retired from boxing with a record of 35 wins from 39 fights. He had done an exhibition fight in London with Muhammad Ali, with Ali just having the upper hand, and it had caused a stir in boxing circles. He had tried rugby league in Dewsbury but packed that in when he realised that all he wanted to do was fight. Gardner was suicidal in the Canary Islands, and Roy took a weapon from him to help save his life. Gardner went back to Newcastle, where he was stabbed 14 times but survived, and ended up selling franking machines.

While Roy was making and selling jewellery, and trying to go straight, his 18-year-old wife Anthea was unhappy. He had 'an old-fashioned attitude about her getting a job', i.e. old Roy thought she should stay at home and do housewifey things, and she did not. He paid for cosmetic surgery on her nose he said (he didn't), and bought her two horses (one allegedly worth £1,800) and a Mercedes-Benz. But she said 'the age gap was already beginning to show'. The early '80s were a busy time for him. They had been married in February '84 at Croydon registry office, on the same weekend that an unsuspecting Renate Blauel married Elton John.

I have seen pictures of the wedding. They're in a wood-panelled room cutting a two-tier cake covered in white icing. She's in a modern, off-white dress, he's in a cream-coloured single-breasted suit with a white carnation in his buttonhole. It's a classic '80s snap and everyone looks happy, apart from her father, David, who is wearing a slightly forced smile. The bride has a great smile. There's an obligatory 'hold hands and cut the cake' shot, like everyone who gets married is so inseparable they have to hold the knife together. I don't know why photographers do that. Anyway, from the nice surroundings (it looks like a stately home), the bride and groom had a table booked at what a guest described as a 'spit and sawdust' venue in Smithfield Market, London. The train robbers who had attended had been asking where it was, and Roy was coy, not wanting them to gatecrash, presumably.

They eventually ended up in a restaurant with a kind of minstrels' gallery above where, unsurprisingly, many of the train robbers and others from London's criminal fraternity were looking down and laughing. They had hired a rough-looking erotic dancer in shabby clothes (note to self; must call my ex-wife) to lap dance for him. She sang a clever ditty about Roy and the robbers and, from what I was told, everyone had a great, if somewhat unconventional, party. Roy loved fun, and practical jokes, and he laughed loudly and often. These glimpses are precious to me. It shows someone away from the formality of the racing crowd, that racing crowd he was so keen to fit in with, and he seems more relaxed with the world.

Just one month before this, Roy was acquitted of VAT fraud in a major criminal case. Anthea knew it, and about the train robbery, but had come to work for him and they genuinely fell in love. I learned that Anthea was a fan of Roy's from afar, perhaps even from when he was inside for the train robbery. The marriage papers show him as a jeweller and her as a secretary. There was a 30-year age gap. Brodie nicknamed her Griselda and he also claims to have gate-crashed their honeymoon in Crete and told another utterly unprintable anecdote about a leper colony. Roy's new father-in-law was a NatWest employee and there is no record of his opinion of his colourful son-in-law who, he would certainly have known, was by then a career criminal.

Chapter 14 – '83, Fingered by Leonard

In '83-ish, many miles from Roy, 'name' (from much earlier in this book) paid a builder to construct a lovely, large house. The one with views. Now this might be a coincidence, but at the same time, Roy was earning so much money that he was struggling to use it. I have heard figures of a quarter of a million pounds per week for a very small, focused gang, who were committing VAT fraud on a massive scale. His friend Charlie Wilson was somehow involved, and a fellow called Raj from Hatton Garden who, I've learned, scarpered to Pakistan when the ruse was rumbled. Armed robber Jamie Redmond was also in the gang.

Perhaps a forensic accountant could untangle the numbers, but I am perhaps 1% convinced that Roy's money ended up funding name's big house. 'Name' had money of their own, but some things tied up. What Roy did with the money is less interesting than how he 'earned' it. There was a method of buying legitimate gold, then melting it down in a smelter, before selling it as virgin gold and getting a new hallmark, and doing so under a newly created company that vanished before the VAT was payable on the revenue. I think there may be a simpler way of explaining it, but that's the gist of it. This had been happening on a small scale already in and around Hatton Garden's jewellery businesses, and so the idea wasn't an original one, but Roy and Charlie just did it on a much, much larger scale.

So successful was this business that they were actively buying gold from the public and using that in their scheme, too. Customs and Excise ran covert operations with names such as Argonaut, Leonard, Finger and Ernie. Leonard was the operation that snared Roy. They were accused of avoiding (stealing) £2.4 million in taxes. That's almost the same amount as the train robbery. Tax fiddles put me in mind of Bernie, who hadn't responded to my letter, so I followed up with another.

Dear Mr Ecclestone,

I wrote to you recently asking about your memories of the racing driver, Roy James, you may remember. I had enclosed a stamped addressed envelope, but as you've not written back to me, can I ask that you at least return the stamp?

Yours hopefully,

Richard von Duisberg

Roy's friends from this era will say that his crimes did not have victims, as such. Robbery from the state, banks and big institutions was fine. Anything else was 'beneath him'. Perhaps this mindset explains why so many people, to this day, still have a romantic view of the Great Train Robbery and criminals who conduct such crimes. The same people, I would wager, will let rip on social media about tax-dodging celebrities and about potholes and underfunded schooling. A friend in the CID told me that, if they couldn't get enough evidence to secure a criminal conviction, they'd pass their case details to the tax authorities who were 'far 'arder than we are'. Today, we have unexplained wealth orders and other financial and legal devices.

Back then, police corruption was rife, particularly in London. I've listened to stories about how the police of the time would collaborate with such crooks in return for money and favours and so on. I bribed a Moroccan policeman once for a minor traffic offence because 'pretty English boy, very nice [in] prison'. €20 to save my modesty seemed like a wise move. Roy's accomplice, Charlie Wilson, cut what I think is called a sweetheart deal to pay some taxes and, I heard, the jury was 'nobbled' when gay jurors were photographed romancing in a hotel together. The case crawled to a stalemate and the gang was lucky to get off.

Roy was held on remand for quite some time over the VAT fiddle and was very angry about it when he was eventually released. You or I might think, having actually stolen a huge sum of money, that a short spell in jail awaiting trial, and then being acquitted, is a small price to pay. But Roy was very angry and it gives an insight into his thought processes. In his mind, as he was not found guilty, he should not have been held at all. This was, to him, a huge injustice. It took me some time to appreciate this perspective.

'Name' denies any knowledge of these crimes when I asked them, despite one of their very own letters complaining about the cost of parking being printed in the newspapers at the same time as the reports of the VAT crime. 'Name' was a prolific nuisance at the time, poking authorities about subjects such as fish offal and the aesthetics of electricity pylons. Nobbling was a real issue in the legal system, then. There was a remarkable instance I came across in my research of one of the train robbery gang having to bribe a policeman to make an arrest where the policeman had already been bribed to *not* make the arrest. Criminals literally paying for the law to be enforced.

What first caught my attention about Roy was the fact that he was once a racing driver. '79 marked the end of his attempts to make a proper fist of it as a racer. He was 44 years old. Looking at the latest Formula One grid, of the 20 drivers, Roy would have been old enough to be the father of half of them. On 15th and 16th September 1979, Roy raced at Phoenix Park in Dublin in Formula Ford, driving something called a Hawke DL19. This car was described as being fast and neutral to drive, and 'stops on a dime'. It was designed by a Lotus Formula One mechanic and all-round good egg called David Lazenby. Others driving a Hawke included Irishman Derek Daly (now living in the US) and Britain's Derek Warwick – both went onto Formula One and were very successful drivers. Roy was old enough to be their father. If this sounds like sour grapes, then yes, it probably is.

Roy achieved more in motorsport, even in his last season, than I've ever done. I once completed a rally stage in France, arriving at the finish line after all the organisers had left, which I partially blame on my navigator, my 10-year-old daughter who had 'accidentally' drunk some complimentary champagne, which got me bollocked by her mother when we got home. I did once win a trophy in some endurance racing in America, but the plywood 'judges choice' trophy was the motoring equivalent of the 'well done' sticker that sports teachers used to give to the lazy kid just for remembering to bring his PE kit. I've got one of those somewhere, too. Roy's Hawke ended up in the hands of a John Anderson, I think, who raced it at Donington Park.

I love tracing these old cars and seeing them in action today, when I can. Racing marked a sort of parallel universe for Roy, a place where he could shed his notoriety and just enjoy himself. Max Moseley told a similar story of how he enjoyed motorsport when people didn't (at first, anyway) associate his name with that of his fascist father. By complete coincidence, Moseley lived on a farm that was very, very close to the scene of the Great Train Robbery. You can see why some people jump to conclusions. I do not have a record of Roy's finish in this race in '79 in Ireland, but he was listed as car 1 in heat 1 of the Formula Ford event on page 67 of the rather lovely 85-page programme. There is no mention of his story anywhere, although there could be something on page 73, which is in Gaelic. I believe he crashed out but I hope that Roy enjoyed his last competitive race without his past overshadowing him.

The programme is full of adverts for Ford Capris, car stereos, Minis and places like the French Connection disco, 'Dublin's newest night spot, jackets compulsory'. I love this. I get great voyeuristic pleasure in delving into this era. Adverts for cassette players, cigarettes, oil. I buy copies of old magazines to build up a better understanding of racing from this time. I even read the classifieds. In one mag, there's an advert from James Hunt selling some of his own cars with his home phone number listed. Can you imagine Max Verstappen sticking his old belongings on eBay with his mobile number, now that he's old enough to get his own place? 'For sale, my scooter and Xbox, buyer to collect.' I swear I can smell the glorious past in these fusty old magazines. I want to open the pages and dive in, face first, to a different time. I succeed only in getting a weird paper cut on my face.

Chapter 15 – '79, Hitler is a little shit

While Roy was enjoying his last weekend of racing in '79, his fellow train robbers had a reunion. The photographs make them look rather awkward. That summer, the gang had been promoting a book about the train robbery, this one authored by Piers Paul Read and, supposedly, 'their story'. Read might be a multi-award winning author and Fellow of the Royal Society of Literature, but the book is pants. The kind of pants that live in the lost and found box at schools that lazy kids who 'forget' their PE kit are forced to wear – pants with someone else's skid marks in (and if that sentence doesn't get me a literary award, then I'm going to take hostages). The publishers went to great lengths to promote the book, which, reportedly, the gang members were each paid £10k to support. In June of '79, the publisher tried to place adverts for the book on the matchboxes in British Rail's buffet cars. BR said no as it was tasteless and it made the news anyway.

I have bought and read the book. There's a thread running through it that should be not just comic sans but comic sans in bold. There's a prevailing mystery about who the brains and funding was behind the Great Train Robbery when, in fact, they were a clever bunch who mostly came up with the idea themselves. Anyway, the gang (including Roy) decided that, if the book sold enough copies, someone would make a film about it, and that they'd earn a healthy cut from the proceeds. So they came up with the Nazi thread, and nobody likes Nazis, not even David Brodie, who described Hitler in his book as 'a little shit'.

The gang decided, without the author's knowledge, to claim that Otto Skorzeny was the man who funded the robbery. Skorzeny had a huge scar across his face from a fencing incident and has the mad, unrepentant look of a man who joined the Nazis in '32. His war exploits aren't going to be repeated here, but he cleverly dodged the noose in his trial as a war criminal, escaped and allegedly helped up to 600 officers of the SS escape to South America, South Africa and elsewhere after the war. We can say with complete, irrefutable certainty that he never won a Blue Peter badge. The gang concocted some 'evidence' and got support from Skorzeny's wife, which the author must have quickly sussed but mentions anyway because Nazis sell books (not literally; I'm not *that* upset at the lack of a publishing deal for the thing in your hands).

Read went all the way to Brazil to find that this part of the robbers' story was a hoax; a 5,764-mile flight from London, which would cost £21,849, one way, if travelling by Luton DART. Roy said that, originally, they were going to use some Italian count as the bad guy, but they knew some mysterious South African agent who knew Skorzeny's wife and she was game in return for a cut in any future film money. In any case, Roy said that the government banned the film from being made, but it wasn't made because the Nazi-themed version would have been plain silly. From implausible plots to Bristol, may I introduce you to Brian.

In '79, a Mr Brian Carlton was driving his Porsche to Wales with his young wife, Sian, in the passenger seat, to see his in-laws. Crashing through the central reservation came a Mercedes-Benz, which hit them head-on, tragically killing Brian Carlton and his wife instantly. Sian would have died probably not knowing that her husband was previously known as Brian Field, having changed his name to escape his past. Brian was a bent solicitor who had been part of the Great Train Robbery and had botched his role. He was a wealthy man, owning a beautiful home in a remote corner of Cornwall, having worked for many criminals to help create false alibis and other manufactured evidence to help them. He died a fast, accidental death after having previously dodged it many times. Brian was a wanted man by many of his ex-customers.

Considering it was over 20 years since the crime, the Great Train Robbery still stirred emotions in the public, in the '70s. Author Read, plugging the Nazi book in '78, helped to set up an event at Cambridge University where students were encouraged to debate the robbery. The gang dutifully turned up in Jaguars, looking every inch like London gangsters, but barely 100 students attended.

It was the weekend of the Oxford vs. Cambridge cricket match, which had been delayed to accommodate this debate and caused annoyance at the university. Some smart-arses in the audience booed and hissed and questioned Read about the morality of earning money off the back of a crime and about paying tax, and then generally misbehaved. The robbers laughed it off, Roy included. They appreciated the anarchy and were probably getting fed up at being dragged around to sell a story.

Roy deployed whataboutism and made a point to the audience that no one was seemingly bothered about a Hungarian crime circle recently convicted of a worldwide fraud. 'Investors may have committed suicide because of them', he said. Since when did Roy care about banks and investors? That crime was compared in court to the Great Train Robbery. Judge Gerald Hines said the crime was one of 'immense gravity' and The Washington Post said it 'could have wrecked the entire banking system of the Western World', which I reckon would have appealed to Roy and anyone on the 0732 from Leicester to London trying to use the First Direct app.

The man behind this 'Hungarian fraud' was Henry Oberlander (a Czech with many, many other aliases), and his gang included an Argentinian forger, a Soho bookie, an English squash player and a Nazi tank commander. All good stories should have a Nazi in it, as I learned from Piers Paul Read's book. I look forward to similar Nazi themes in print; 'Sherlock Holmes and the Hun of the Baskervilles' or, for the kids, 'Harry Potter and the Wizard of Berchtesgaden'.

Some newspapers were going to serialise Read's book. Ena Howard (among many others) wrote furiously to her local newspaper, the Liverpool Herald. 'Is it right that these evil men should be assisted to make money from their past misdeeds with your encouragement?' Other headlines shouted 'crime does pay' and 'criminals must not profit from evil', next to adverts for school trousers costing 99p.

Someone who signed off as 'Disgusted 80 year old' threatened to write to their MP. I particularly enjoyed the inane rhetoric from someone writing in to ask 'How do the hospital doctors feel who read this?' A Mrs. Beaumont wrote in to cancel her subscription, but you just know that she'd buy a copy anyway in the hope of seeing her letter in print, the daft old bat.

Sometime around '78, a friend says he took Roy back to Bridego Bridge and that he didn't recognise it until the last minute. Bushes had grown. Things had moved. He pointed out where he'd parked, and driven, but was uncomfortable. Roy said 'It's as if it didn't happen to me... I feel kind of sick at the way things turned out, what a staggering waste.' The media were still dogging him, too. He defensively told the press 'I have never been on social security.' Why would you, Roy? You'd not long before committed the biggest robbery in British history! There was other nonsense about having bought a large house but someone else stole the deeds. Money seemed to slip through his fingers, but it's hard to unpick the truth from Roy's stories at times. Was he genuinely remorseful at the things he had done or was he just feeling sorry for himself?

This same friend asked, perhaps overestimating my connections, if I'd ever spoken to Bernie about Roy. I was still keen to explore the idea that Roy the racer was different to Roy the robber. Bernie was known for occasionally giving a leg-up to people, he said. Maybe he'd give me a leg-up, too. I mentioned my postal correspondence, which got a laugh, and prompted me to send one last follow-up.

Dear Mr Ecclestone,

Further to earlier correspondence, I now realise the financial short-sightedness of me writing to you to ask for the return of my stamped addressed envelope. I had spent 75 pence in order to attempt to recover 75 pence. Indeed, sending this third letter at a further cost of 75 pence puts me into the red to the sum of £2.25. Can I please ask you to return my original stamp, so I may at least reduce my overall loss to a more manageable £1.50.

Yours, etc.

Richard von Duisberg

Chapter 16 – '77, Racing for Holland

The top tier of motorsport is (sit *down*, NASCAR fans) Formula One. Beneath that is Formula Two and then, unsurprisingly, Formula Three. Formulas Two and Three emerged from the Formula Junior world where Roy's reputation as a racer stemmed from. In '77, aged 42, he was still working to get a drive in a competitive race seat in some semi-professional capacity, but age and possibly reputation was against him. He was going to be paired with Dutch rising star, Jan Lammers, who was just 21. Lammers later won the 24 Hours of Le Mans, did a few seasons in Formula One and was an incredible talent in different racing disciplines.

There must have been motorsport industry help to even get Roy into this position. A privateer could not just pay their way into this level at a time when racing was (thanks Bernie) becoming a professional, money-making empire. I emailed Jan Lammers and crossed my fingers for a response. In an interesting parallel with Roy's life, Lammers later took a 10-year sabbatical from Formula One, although he wasn't locked up for being a wrong 'un, he was 'Racing for Holland' in a sports-car series. Jan then returned to Formula One with March in '92.

Roy would have loved a break like that. The police still idly followed him, his reputation as 'The Weasel' seemingly unshakeable. My scruffy notes say that, around '76/'77, Roy employed a mechanic called Ted Higgins to work on his cars at a lock-up under some railway arches in Camberwell. Today, Camberwell is slowly getting gentrified, but the arches still stand, a short walk from shuttered shops, all-you-can-eat nail bars and places selling Kentucky fried pigeon.

Higgins was described by Motor Sport magazine as 'Mr E's personal mechanic'. The name Mr E sounds like a drug dealer, but I assume it actually means Bernie Ecclestone. Higgins is mentioned as working on a 1983 Brabham BT52 that appeared at the 2023 Goodwood Members' Meeting. Roy's links to Brabham and, therefore, Bernie become a bit stronger than just the trophy-maker story suggests. Bernie bought Brabham in '72 and must have worked with Higgins. I'm going off on a tangent here; we'll come back to Brabham and I hope to track down Higgins for a cuppa someday. In '77, Roy didn't get a drive in Formula Three with Jan but he was still very active in motorsport.

As I'm digesting all this, and wondering if Roy felt desperate by now, trying to find a race seat, I get a few text messages from a Dutch number. 'Can I call you later', followed by 'just at a counter in a shop' and finally 'I try but voicemail'. I call it back and instantly get a jovial Jan Lammers, 'Roy? The guy who robbed the train? I remember him.'

I drink a coffee and make notes as Jan Lammers kindly shares a little of his past with me. He is both straightforward in that way the Dutch are, and also modest, skipping over his personal achievements, which include winning the 24 Hours of Le Mans (I think I mentioned that earlier, but it's a big deal and worth repeating) and twice winning the 24 Hours of Daytona. Jan wants to talk about how much fun it was as a young man, coming from Holland to live in Southend. I want to hear about the racing, even if it's to the detriment of my quest to learn more about our anti-hero, Roy.

Jan's Le Mans race was an epic scrap. 260,000 fans attended to see the tightest finish in a decade, with Jaguar winning by just 180 metres. Lammers and his team had started behind a 1-2-3 line-up of Porsche cars and had to contend with a broken windscreen, rain and a gearbox stuck in 4th. I've been to the British Motor Museum to see the winning car, a Jaguar XJR-9, and my awestruck assessment of 'Cor, it's dead good, just *look* at it!' might explain why I never get a gig writing about racing cars for motorsport publications. This fag-packet-liveried racer is a brute. It has a V12 engine and something called a carbon fibre and Kevlar monocoque. It is capable of 245 mph. It must have been exhausting to drive. I'm knackered just looking at it.

Jan kindly brings me back on track. He was very polite, explaining that he didn't remember much about the possible deal to pair him, the young, European hot shoe, with Roy, the old-timer with an iffy background. He did remember Roy as being a 'competitive driver' in '77, which is quite the compliment considering that, within barely a year of that assessment, Jan would go on to win the European Formula Three Championship (the first Dutchman do to so) and springboard from there straight into Formula One. The closest Roy got to a cup in '78 was seeing some of his prison-made silverware on display at the Prison Art exhibition at the Highland Tolbooth church during the Edinburgh Festival. Jan tells me that the Great Train Robbery made the news all over the Netherlands, and Roy arriving at the Formula Ford festival made quite an impression on him. I tried to read an article about the robbery in the Dutch language newspaper, De Telegraaf, which enticed me with 'Krijgonbeperkttoegangtot alle artikelenvanaf €0,99 per week' which is Dutch for 'paywall, you cheapskate'.

I asked Jan about how he got started in racing; 'At the Slotemaker skid school', he said, which sounds far, far cooler when pronounced with a Dutch accent instead of an English one. 'Then I started to race Simcas.' I now want to own a Simca. In an attempt to find some common ground, I excitedly told Jan that I'd driven at his home circuit of Zandvoort, although the sparkle of this revelation was somewhat tarnished when I admitted it was in a rented Opel Corsa and I later received a warning for trespass. Our call comes to an end.

Lammers' Le Mans win was shared with teammate, Johnny Dumfries, who, you might remember from earlier in this book, is formally known as the Marquess of Bute, cousin of the shady Charles Crichton-Stuart, who failed to find Saudi customers for Roy's 'acquired' jewellery later in the '80s. Time talking with Jan confirms my recently formed theory that many of the people associated with Roy from motorsport seem to be straightforward to deal with, whereas the rest of 'em are often (but not always) dodgy. It also indicates that most of the motorsport people are seemingly unaware that Roy shot his father-in-law, hid firearms under the lawn and was keen to share tips on the disposal of bodies. Not that I tell them this. They can read this book and find out for themselves, that's my paywall.

Chapter 17 – '77, Hotdog

In '77, Roy bought a Formula Ford car from Derek Warwick. I managed to track him down in the Channel Islands for a chat about his time racing and his experience with Roy. Derek is described as 'the best driver never to have won a Grand Prix' and it was fantastic to talk with someone I watched as a kid. Ayrton Senna refused to have Derek as a teammate at Lotus in later years in Formula One; that's some compliment. Derek recalled the transaction, discussions around cash and Roy saying he needed to be 'whiter than white' when buying Derek's car. They shared a hotdog at Silverstone, with Roy looking over his shoulder, confident but cagey. His reputation, by that point, preceded him, and there was the feeling that the fraud squad or some other authority was watching, waiting for him to slip up.

Roy paid by cheque, all above board, and although he was in his 40s at that point, Derek said he had the feeling that he was still quick and had probably been 'bloody quick' back in his day. Derek clearly liked Roy. The train robbery was a story from another lifetime then, and Roy comes over as a lovable rogue to those who mingled with him in motorsport in the '70s. Derek had done well in Formula Ford, winning 33 races and the European Championship, as well as finishing 2nd in three other main UK Championships. His book (which should go to print soon after this one) is called 'Never Look Back'. He's a focused sort of chap, as you'd expect from an ex-top-flight racing driver, and he explained that, after Formula Ford, he was only focused on the next step, which was Formula Three, and (as it happens) he would be mixing it in Formula One only a few years after that.

He drove for Brabham towards the end of the 'Bernie era' there. Derek said he regrets not knowing more about Roy at the time, but the Weasel was a secretive sort of man. Derek later sends me an email to confirm what we've discussed.

'Like I said I the phone I have a very limited memory of Roy James other than being star struck being one of the great train robbers and bought my formula Ford. I meet Roy James in the paddock at Brands Hatch, you instantly liked him because of his outgoing character and funny stories. He had something about him and you found yourself hug on every word, what made it more mysterious was you knew that they were police or someone over his shoulder all the time.'

If Roy was the Weasel, then his dad was a rat. Not 'The Rat', Niki Lauda's nickname, or some gangster name, but a rat in the derogatory sense. On 16th October 1977, Sidney George James died aged 71, in Stepney, London. Sid James (not *that* Sid James, who had himself carked it the previous year) was Roy's father. The only personal recollection I have recorded anywhere about Roy and his father is from Brodie's memory that Roy called his father 'a rat, that's all there is to say about him'. And that's it. It seems they had been estranged for very many years, although Sid will not have been able to avoid his son's name in the media. He could not have been a wealthy man. Roy himself did not drink or smoke. We also know that he took a dim view of his wife's drinking too. Roy's father had walked out on the family when Roy was young, and it's likely that the old man was a bit of a boozer.

Stepney was, according to the following lazy copy/paste from The London Encyclopaedia, '... built up rapidly in the 19th century, mainly to accommodate immigrant workers and displaced London poor, and developed a reputation for poverty, overcrowding, violence and political dissent.' Thanks for that. To nick someone else's work again, there's a great line in Lock, Stock and Two Smoking Barrels about the area; 'Handmade in Italy, hand-stolen in Stepney.' There is no record of Roy having any dealings with his father, nor can I find anyone who knew Roy who remembers them having any contact. I have a suspicion that, even though he was born in a place called Street, Devon, and baptised soon after in London, his father may have been from an Irish family, for clues I later find.

The '76/'77 era saw Roy scrapping in various cars at UK circuits and titbits of misinformation were lazily left around for me to find years later. There's a photograph of him driving a 'Hawke RP21 car', which is probably actually a Brabham because it has their Motor Racing Developments name plastered down the side, at a race at 'Croft', which couldn't be Croft because I've read the race programme front to back and back again and he's not listed in it. In this picture he's looking tired, which might be explained by him being in a car that isn't the right car at a circuit where he couldn't have been. And on a different date. He was also given a leg-up by circuit owner John Webb, who owned Motor Racing Stables, and crashed out of a race and into a photographer at Brand Hatch. It's confusing for all.

At Croft, in the race he wasn't in, he retired from 9th place says some confused person who probably had a lovely time cheering on the wrong driver. I spent some time untangling this knot to find it was actually Kirkistown, near Belfast, and he raced alongside Divina Galica, who was a rare female entrant in Formula One in later life, and was awarded an MBE. The Belfast Telegraph described him here as 'a charger'. It is Formula Ford stuff Roy was doing, mainly, which is broadly comparable to his old Formula Junior/Formula Three Brabham cars. There was a shadow race series which was briefly popular called Formula Atlantic, which aimed to allow for the performance of Formula Two cars, but in a more driver-friendly Formula Three package. Roy tried to get into any of it, all of it. As we saw Roy's downward trajectory cross with the rocketing Jan Lammers in '77, he also came across future Formula One champ Nigel Mansell.

I once recall a conversation in wonky English with a Brazilian friend who told me that their favourite driver of all time was not Senna, as expected, but 'The Nigel'. I have never heard him described as The Nigel before, but it seems fitting. The Nigel's first race in Formula Ford, around the time he packed in working for Lucas, was at Leicestershire's Mallory Park. He won this race, and five others, in his first season and, in the following season, won 33 of 42 races entered, despite suffering a broken neck. There's a story which says that Roy, never one to back down on track, clattered The Nigel in practice and nearly did for them both. Others who raced against him in this era told the same story of a man who would brake later than everyone, who would give everything, although Brodie reckoned 'Roy didn't know how to turn in', which had me nodding sagely before discretely googling to see what that meant.

With Mallory Park being fairly local to me, I decided to try and get a feel for racing here. Paying a small sum to join a trackday, and driving an ancient, rotten MX-5, I bought a helmet of such poor quality that even scooter riders on Deliveroo duty would decline to wear it. I was curious what £15 had gotten me and got a bit carried away with a screwdriver, so ended up pulling out of the pit lane with bits of polystyrene sticking in my ear. Polystyrene, that's what £15 helmets are made from. That's all that keeps my face from turning to mush if there's an accident, the same material they pack kettles and toasters with.

Trackdays like this are non-competitive and, fortunately, so am I. But charging down to a corner called Gerard's with a narrow focus on a thing Brodie had told me is called an apex, with someone trying to mate his loutish Subaru with my little Mazda, I was reminded that I am not a racing driver. On the back straight, I got a whiff of delicious, mouth-watering bacon. A few minutes later, on that same lap, I thought I might need a wee. I pulled in, telling the concerned marshal that I was concerned about my carbon fibre and Kevlar monocoque, and sat eating a rather agreeable brunch, which took up much of my day. I was in a car slow enough that folks could overtake me, so I'd get some space to myself to feel what it meant to drive quickly on a race track, but not so slow that I'd be a mobile chicane. Probably I was just in everyone's way.

There were perhaps a dozen or so others here, reliving their own driving fantasies. How on earth does a driver in Formula Anything stay focused (and safe) with many dozens of cars of near-identical performance all heaving their way onto the same little bit of tarmac? That's what an apex is, by the way, a little bit of tarmac. When I got home, I threw the helmet, with little balls of polystyrene clinging to it with static, in the recycling bin. On bin day, I discovered that the binmen had, passive aggressively, left the helmet behind on the driveway. I had spent more on bacon and coffee than fuel. Actually, I had spent more on bacon and coffee than helmet. It was fun to follow in Roy's footsteps for the day but I am not The Weasel and I am certainly not The Nigel.

Chapter 18 – '76, Sally

As Roy was visiting various circuits in '76, trying to rediscover his driving mojo, one of his romantic dalliances was hang-gliding, topless, as a publicity stunt. Sally Farmiloe had just appeared in the film Spanish Fly, alongside Terry-Thomas and Leslie Phillips, described by Barry Norman in The Observer as 'the least funny British funny film ever made' and now she's on the South Downs in a bikini. Well, it *was* the '70s, I suppose. I can only conclude that, if you're hang-gliding, topless, then you need bigger kicks in your life than hanging around with a back-of-the-pack racing driver who was not long out of jail.

Sally Farmiloe was, by her own admission to The Sunday Times 'a bit of a wild child'. A couple of years before meeting Roy, and hang-gliding topless, she lived in Chelsea and was convicted of stealing from a store in South Kensington. 'I felt like doing something awful after a boyfriend had left me', she said in her defence, before being fined a tenner. The pictures of '76 show her strapped to a hang-glider, which was in turn suspended by cables and dangled near the edge of a very steep hill in what looks like the South Downs. There's a Rover P6 and a Ford Cortina in the background, and a photographer with flares. You're asking what Shutterstock charge for this memorable image, aren't you? Well it's £29.

More voyeuristic readers than you might say that, compared to the £159 Shutterstock wanted for a picture of Roy in a scruffy jumper, £29 for Sally Farmiloe hang-gliding topless is tremendous value for money. Well, my miniscule budget for creating this book was mostly spent on the Luton DART, Brodie's book and polystyrene PPE. Anyway, it's not that kind of book, but you can google it and peer through the Shutterstock watermark for the most '70s image you'll ever see.

Sally moved on from Roy to get married to someone more sensible than him and worked as an actress, on and off. Sally's father had been a yacht broker and so she stepped comfortably into the cast of the doomed boaty soap opera, Howards Way, before having an affair with Jeffrey Archer, Baron shitbag of Weston-super-Mare.

Late August '76 saw Roy crashing, again, this time at Brands Hatch in Kent, when practicing in a 'Star of Tomorrow' event in Formula Ford. And in April of the same year, he got a drive in a Renault 5 race, set up by the manufacturer, Renault, to help promote their new hatchback. These one-make races were quite popular for a while, a throwback to when manufacturers used racing as a means to promote the reliability and performance of their brand. For a while, I was confused by this Renault 5 race, as it was described in contemporary reports as 'Renault v' with the lower case v throwing me off the scent. What is a Renault vee?

The 5 was to become the best-selling car in France, ever, with over five million made. Renault pitched it as a 'car for all seasons' and a later advertising campaign asked 'what is yours called?' Roy's Renault might have been called 'crashed' or 'written off' as he was trying too hard at Mallory. Roy stuffed the car when lying ninth on lap four. The race organiser had found it hard to find people wanting to join the event, and Roy was perhaps just a 'seat filler'.

As Jan Lammers told me, Roy drove flat out, regardless of consequences, and regularly crashing out was just the logical consequence of this strategy. Roy said that year 'I don't want racing to become a hobby – it's all or nothing.' Motorsport nerds might baulk at this, but that puts Roy in the same 'all or nothing' category of drivers, alongside Schumacher and Senna and one of my favourite Formula One drivers, Romain Grosjean. Grosjean was described by Mark Webber as a 'first-lap nutcase'. I'd had the same words, in reverse order, shouted at me by the marshals when trying to leave Mallory circuit prematurely.

My correspondence with Bernie had yielded nothing more than 'return to sender', which is a pity as it's time in this mooch through Roy's fascinating life to talk about that trophy. Feel free to wander off and make a cup of tea if you've heard this bit many times before; I'll still be droning on when you get back.

Roy was desperate for help getting a re-entry into the world of racing and went to the house of Graham Hill, who was two-time world champion by then. Graham's son, Damon, remembers the occasion and of his dad sending Roy away to try Bernie Ecclestone. Bernie said Roy was too old and he couldn't help recommend him as a driver to anyone, but asked what his trade was. Roy explained he'd trained as a silversmith. Bernie then gave him a commission to make the Formula One Race Promoters' Trophy. This was presented for the first time in May '75 at the Monaco Grand Prix, a race won by Niki Lauda, in which Graham Hill came 21st and retired. As mentioned earlier in this book, that fact is seemingly known by many people, and so it's a good time to recap where we are.

In reverse order; Roy has died, been operated on, plotted a jet-ski drugs trip to the Netherlands, buried a machine gun, fell out with the press, told lies about Nazis, shot his father-in-law, attempted to blow up a safe, tried to go straight, crashed quite a few cars trying to resurrect a career in motorsport and met a topless hang-gliding actress. And that's what we *can* print.

In Titanic movie terms, we have set sail, made a nice pot of tea during the ad breaks and met some colourful people. But we have not yet hit the iceberg in Roy's life. I am grateful for this iceberg because it drew attention to his later life, the bit we've covered already, and made it possible to find resources and references and even people still alive who knew him. I found the son of the court records officer who had dealt with one of his cases, and he was well into his 70s. The Titanic journey is a bit of an awkward metaphor when writing about someone's life, backwards, but I'm juggling writing this and simultaneously listening to a work call on Teams about 'synergies', so you'll have to bear with me. You're on mute, Dave. Dave, you're on mute.

Chapter 19 – '75, Roman numerals joke

Roy's lucky break in his later racing career came in '75, when he was given the chance to drive a Formula Atlantic Lola T360 single seater. The same car could be used in Formula 2 configuration. It's the real thing. It had approximately 200 horsepower, almost twice what Roy might have wrung from his Formula Junior cars over a decade earlier, which was the last time he'd driven competitively. This car was one of a type given as a prize by promoter Wella, who were using motorsport to promote their haircare products.

In the same era, grot mag Penthouse sponsored Hesketh, Durex sponsored Surtees and another Surtees car was sponsored by the bizarre 'Southern Organs' company, which was notionally a church organ restoration company but ended up with some hoods doing a flit to a Scottish island with cash in a briefcase. So, while the top teams had fags and booze money to play with, Roy's scrounged car was shampoo-powered.

It was, only very, very briefly, Roy's car. It belonged to American privateer Ted Wentz, who I had tracked down to a Jeep accessories dealership in Pennsylvania where no one answers the phone. There are a number of Wentz's in that family business and I am not sure if it's Wentz I, Wentz II or Wentz III that I need. The Roman-numerals joke in my voice message left for him may have precluded a response when I asked about 'Wentz eye eye eye'. And then I got sent to America for work and learning what happened with the Formula Atlantic car got a bit easier.

Lotus was one of the leading pioneers in motorsport. Its boss, Colin Chapman, would find new and exciting ways to design a car to give a technical advantage. He would read the rules, find loopholes and push things to the limit. He once read that the bulkhead (a heavy plate separating engine and driver) must be made of metal. This makes sense because, if there's a fire, or something flies off at speed, the driver needs protecting. But Chapman wanted to save weight, so mixed some aluminium powder in with some paint, daubed it all over a thin piece of cardboard and tried to pass that off as a 'metal' bulkhead. Chapman's cars were light and fast and sometimes lethal. Key components would be designed to perform two purposes. The chassis carries the driver but might have the engine mounted straight to it, that sort of thing. And I use this philosophy in my day job today. Each thing I do (e.g. go to America) will serve at least two purposes (work meeting and huge detour to track down ol' eye eye).

In my haste to do two things at once, I was in a rush to check out of a hotel near New York. It was very hot, I was very jet-lagged and I'm clearly making excuses for what happened next.

The friendly guy on the desk was Mexican and his name badge said Pedro. I had prepaid and just wanted a copy of the invoice. I said hello amigo and asked for the invoice, please. There was a delay, so I made a bit of small talk. He heard my accent. 'Where you from?' he asked. 'England' I said. 'I like England accent.' Bit of an awkward pause. 'How's your day going?' I asked. 'OK'... longer pause. He then felt obliged to say something. 'I love your culture' he said. By now, I'm a bit fed up waiting for this invoice and he's making no attempt to print anything. 'Thanks...have you been to England?' He had not. 'So what part of English culture do you like?' I asked, putting him on the spot a bit. Very, very long pause now. Some people behind start forming a queue. Still he doesn't give me the invoice. 'Errrrrr......' he says, then triumphantly...'the clock, the clock!' ...I assume he means Big Ben. 'Yes, it's impressive.' Still no invoice.

I am feeling cheeky. 'Just the clock? Is that all you like?' I smile at him. Mild panic now sets in as this guy wracks his brains about English culture. 'Theeeee... the, errr......' A massive pause... He forms a bridge shape with his hands... 'THE BRIDGE! THE BRIDGE!'... Oh yes, Tower Bridge, but he's still not printing the bloody invoice. 'Is it just the architecture you like? There's more to English culture, y'know.' I am hot and narked. 'How about the Queen, the Beatles, Stonehenge, Formula One, the terrible food... 'I ask – he doesn't notice the joke, so I put him on the spot. 'Nothing else in English culture take your fancy then?!'... He actually scratches his head. I hear people behind me tutting and don't care.

There's now a pause longer than an X Factor winner announcement. He looks around for help; none comes. 'What else, then?' He finally lights up, Eureka!...'The fish! The fry fish!'...Fish and chips, lovely, yes mate. I love them too. Then feeling bad, and no sign of my invoice, I joke 'You should work for the English tourist board...come and see the clock and the bridge and eat the fried fish! There's not much else worth seeing anyway...'He looks confused. I feel bad. He looks down at the desk – he'd printed my invoice ages ago and I hadn't noticed. Sorry Pedro. I am an arse. And so to Quadratec, Ted's business, and some answers to what happened at Roy's test drive.

Ted spent 6 years in England. 'It was the only place in the world to go if you wanted to race', he told me. He lived in a rented flat in Hammersmith, overlooking the Thames. He was having the time of his life. Promoter David Mills convinced Ted to give up his car to let Roy have a drive as a promotional stunt at Silverstone, aiming for a triumphant return for the Weasel. He was almost a foot shorter and didn't fit in the seat, nor could he manage the controls comfortably. It had twice the power he was used to and he was over-eager to impress onlookers. He hadn't driven a car with proper aero before, nor one on such fat tyres which needed heat before you could really drive fast. You can see where this is going, can't you?

Roy ignored Ted's kindly advice, and that of Lola mechanic Neil Marshall, and soon crashed the car and broke his leg. Roy said at the time, 'My times were coming down nicely and I'd have had a decent position on the grid. After 12 years, it felt good and I was elated. I can't wait to have a go again.' The car was a write-off. 'Time is not on my side', he said, 'I can't afford to miss a day.' Wentz got a Lola development car for the rest of the season and said it was a 'silver lining', as it was way better than the car Roy wrecked. Only the instrument binnacle was worth saving, and it sits on Ted's desk to this day. He didn't let Roy have another go. Mills, who set the whole thing up, later said 'I was asked to help him by all sorts of people in the business' and 'He was a nice enough chap, outgoing, many people liked him and felt he had served more than enough time.' Like others, Mills was happy to see Roy back in a car and issued a press release saying 'Roy James returns to racing!'

At this point in my writing about the Weasel, a moderate dose of paranoia crept in. I sit typing this on a scrounged laptop, scrunched up on a plane. I often forget to save, and then rewrite chunks of it, not saving to the cloud as that's a works account and I get into enough trouble in my 9 to 5 already.

Brodie sends me a text message about something funny but confusing. Then my YouTube playlist starts to throw in more and more adverts because I'm too cheap to pay for the ad-free version. Every time I try and play some punk to get my writing going, I get an advert for Grammarly and someone tries to sell me something in a know-all American voice and undermines my confidence in my writing. I think this may come from me clicking on an advert on Instagram and then buying something, and now my computer knows everything about me.

To remedy this I spill a large amount of coffee on the laptop, then drop it for good measure, but then realise I hadn't saved or clouded it, or whatever, and for that reason, I have typed this last bastard paragraph at least twice now. I then get another very, very polite reminder from 'Name' not to name them or mention where their mansion is.

I am dealing with some colourful people, writing this book. A police friend warned that, as I dig deeper into Roy's story, there'd be people 'wanting a slice'. I naively thought that cake with a coffee would be a reasonable payment in return for information on our anti-hero, then wondered if it meant I was going to get stabbed, before calming down when it just meant that people might want money for helping me, which is easy to deal with because I don't have any. To get a bit of mental reassurance that telling this story backwards made sense, I looked for other examples of reverse-chronology biographies and came across Martin Amis' bleak Time's Arrow, which left me in a bit of a rubbish mood for a while.

This in your hands is a self-published work, to go alongside my book about car factory cock-ups and another about glove puppets working in call centres, which didn't sell many copies. Maybe I should YouTube my work instead of writing. I dunno. My YouTube suggestions keep throwing up the video I made years ago, which is becoming almost as annoying as the preppy Grammarly hipster with his stupid hat and dazzling teeth who appears on almost every single song I try to play. Because of my recent train adventures, I am also getting adverts for a rail company, which I will call £ast M1d!@nd5 Tr41n$ in case the computer works out what I'm typing and sends me even more adverts. Enough navel-gazing, let's get back to the Weasel [hits save].

Chapter 20 – '75, 12p

On 15th August '75, after nearly 12 years in jail, Roy was released. He was collected from Long Lartin jail by someone called John in a smart, new BMW 5 Series. The rumour is that Roy had paid for this car but I never saw him drive it again. He was a Jaguar man when he was choosing. The press were there to capture the moment he drove away from being locked up with the likes of Charlie Kray, elder brother of t'other Krays (not sure why I slipped into Yorkshire there) and John Straffen, who holds the record of being the longest incarcerated prisoner in British history. He had been sentenced to death, which was then commuted to life imprisonment. Perhaps in modern times he would have received the help he needed, as he was assessed as having had a mental age of six. He had hated the police since childhood for reasons no one understood. He had escaped from Broadmoor and killed a girl, telling police who caught him 'I did not kill her' before they'd even told him anyone was dead. He spent 55 years in jail for three murders. Roy used to give Straffen chicken, a prized meal in jail, to keep him happy after Straffen started staring at him. Roy must have been elated to be free.

Roy had served 12 years of his 30-year sentence and, wisely, had realised that avoiding kicking and fighting against the prison system was the way to the quickest exit. 'This is my lucky day', he said, before jovially grumbling about the 12p cost of an ice cream.

Times had changed. There were three million more people living in the UK in '75 than there had been when he went inside. The price of beer and cigarettes had stayed the same, which was of no use to Roy who didn't use either, but the price of a house had gone from £2,700 to nearly £10,000. The prices of ordinary cars roughly doubled in the same period. And inflation wasn't the only problem. Roy's finances had been hit from many directions during his prison time.

The obvious drain on his money was payments made to the likes of John who collected him from jail, who probably charged enough for collecting him to buy the slick BMW he was driving that day. Others, many others, all needing payments to keep quiet, to keep busy and for reasons that Roy couldn't manage from the high-security jails he was in. You can't call the police in such situations and the people you're dealing with are forceful, violent types. Anyone who knew Roy knew he'd robbed millions and charged him accordingly. In addition to that, his mother, Violet, had simply stored all the cash he gave her. None of it was invested. She lived in a flat in Kingston upon Thames, bought for her by Roy, and continued to work as a shop assistant in Bentalls. Roy's crime had burdened her. She led a simple life and worried about people watching her.

In '63, UK interest rates were around zero, and by the '70s, it peaked at almost 25%. I'm more Marc Riley than Rachel Riley, but my primitive grasp of numbers makes me think Roy's money was losing an average of perhaps 10% of its value, year on year, during his incarceration. And now he licked an ice cream in the sun while the Daily Mirror photographer snapped away.

He was wearing a single-breasted pinstriped suit with matching waistcoat, a neat tie, pocket square and cufflinks. Very dapper. Roy and his cornet made page 5 of the paper in what was a slow news day. The publication 'Italian Gelato' says that, today, where I live in the Midlands is the cheapest place to buy ice cream. Two quid buys two scoops, they say. Today, Roy's 12p wouldn't cover sprinkles or even 'raz' (raspberry sauce, sorry; I keep going Yorkshire for some reason).

From Long Lartin, Roy and his man John drove to Highgate where (depending on which of my coffee-stained notes I follow) either the driver paid for two prostitutes or Brodie paid for two prostitutes, and someone haggled them down because [unprintable antisemitism]. He briefly did all the things a man who had been locked up for a very long time could be expected to do. He went shopping, saw his mother and went to the cinema, where he may have seen the recently released classic 'Jaws', which my elderly relative (mentioned at the beginning of this book)remembered as 'Jumbo the whale'.

Hang-gliding into this scene, metaphorically, not literally, comes Sally Farmiloe. They were reported as 'hanging out together'. The late, great, Mrs. Merton (Caroline Ahern) might have asked Sally 'what first attracted you to the millionaire, Roy James?' She was a publicity magnet and (as mentioned earlier) self-confessed wild child, and while Roy wasn't an attention-seeker, he could not have objected to having her on his arm.

Roy went to the gym often, trying to maintain a schedule he'd kept in jail. An old Formula Junior friend, Rodney Banting, said he was supremely fit and worked out every day. He had, said Rodney, 'Olympic levels of fitness.' He and Sally were clearly on very different trajectories; he was heading back to racing and Sally went to Dubai to set up a business selling hot pants. I think that this hot pants 'business', like the hang-gliding, was a bit of mischief conjured up by her and the media together in pursuit of publicity.

Roy then took a step which sort of buggered up this book's title. It was originally to be titled 'Looking for The Weasel'. Then I find that Roy had contacted the press in '75 and, as reported in the Western Daily Press and elsewhere, angrily told them 'Weasel is not my name!' I wasn't sure if this was him trying to throw off his past, to jettison the nickname with such negative connotations, the name which makes such a convenient book title. So I spoke to his old friend, Brodie, who confirmed 'oh yeah, he detested that name' and then sends me a text about skiing in an entirely unrelated matter.

This bombshell has me double and triple checking, before concluding that, no, Roy wasn't the Weasel. So now I go back through my manuscript so far and throw in a dozen or so uses of 'real' to tidy up. 'Looking for The *Real* Weasel' is now my title, although having written 20,000 words and rather enjoying myself, I am going to stick with my original protagonist.

Actually, there are other weasels. An American TV character with the catchphrase 'Hey, buddy', a Canadian comedian whose real name is Wezl, a rock band called Screeching Weasel (fronted by a Ben Weasel), a Norman adventurer who died in 1085 and mafia mobster Jimmy Fratianno, who got his nickname when someone spotted him scarpering from the police and shouted 'look at that weasel run!' Weasel, some gorblimey type in the East End told me, is also Cockney rhyming slang for weasel and stoat, meaning coat. Maybe the *real*, real Weasel (i.e. not ours) got his name from his choice of outer garments. Anyway, if you feel misled by this book's amended title, then I hope you at least feel consoled by the amount of Nazis, nudity and jet-ski smuggling in it so far.

Chapter 21 – '71, The Welsh language Liverpool Daily Echo

Just before his release, Roy had been allowed out on day release. This was in the spring and summer of '75. He wandered around Evesham. This was the first taste of freedom he had had since Christmas of '63. The world had changed. When he was born, people flew biplanes; when he was released, Concorde was breaking the speed of sound. In April '71, he had been downgraded from a category A to a category B prisoner, which had allowed him a bit more of a life inside. He made a silver and pewter cup and saucer, which went to auction a couple of years ago, and a bracelet with his own motto 'nil desperandum' (never despair, to the non-Latin speakers among us). His mate Rodney Banting somehow got £1,000 of silver to Roy inside. He wasn't allowed any tools, despite being a lower-risk prisoner, so he had to make his own. Then fellow prisoners complained about his noisy banging and bashing and he was obliged to set up shop in the toilets. The prison governor confirmed that making such trinkets was acceptable, although added a disclaimer 'prisoners are not allowed to make things such as machine guns', the spoilsport.

As I find the hard facts to build the timeline of Roy's life, such as those above, I also started to hear stories of his capers. He told a tale about his time at Long Lartin involving Scotsmen tunnelling out of the jail and under a football pitch, and the governor finding the hole and falling in. He found this riotously funny. There's no hard record of this ever happening, but I suppose it's not the sort of thing that makes the papers. I couldn't see how he, as someone avoiding trouble, towards the end of his sentence, would be actually on the spot to see someone fall down an escape tunnel. Looking at the jail, it's probably 30 m from the wing nearest to the recreational area and, from there, maybe another 100 m to the main fence and freedom. Were people really digging out of jails in England in the '70s? It sounds like the plot of the film (Roy liked films) 'Escape to Victory', released in '81, around the time the person who told me all this was regularly socialising with Roy. It seems fishy but who *hasn't* talked up a story in the pub? But I can't let it go. I then find document HO 391/369 in the National Archives in Kew, with the startling title 'Investigation into possible escape attempt by inmates: HM Prison Long Lartin, Evesham, Worcestershire' with dates and info that tally with Roy's.

His prison time roughly matches the career of Graham Hill. Hill was slightly older than Roy but got into racing a little later in life. He got the bug through Formula 3 and won his first drivers' championship around the same time Roy and co. were plotting the Great Train Robbery in '62. By the time Roy was out, Hill was retiring. The pain of this, the lost time, must have hurt more than anything else.

Roy was living for the thrill of racing and, reading the race reports in the few magazines he was allowed in his cell, he would have seen Hill win the championship twice and come runner-up three times. The 'what if' scenario is easily overplayed, but it's impossible not to conclude that Roy would have achieved greater things in racing had he stayed on the straight and narrow, and that he would have known this, sat alone in his cell. In addition to this, he was hugely upset to receive back an engagement ring from Miss X, someone from earlier in his life. Getting the ring back was bad enough, but the precious stone had been swapped for a smaller one. Hey, are you feeling sorry for him at this point?

Roy had plenty of female friends. In his last year inside, I came across a letter he had sent to 'The Doghouse Owners' Club'. Every year, a group of racing drivers' wives, partners and girlfriends had a Christmas bash. Roy sent a donation to them every year, once with a note in saying 'Sorry – I cannot be with you due to unforeseen circumstances.' I eventually met the president, Shirley Procter, who knew Roy well. More digging and very many nights squinting at old newspapers on the brilliant and only occasionally broken British Newspaper Archive website throws up more contacts, more stories and further evidence that Roy might have accidentally acquired the nickname 'The Weasel', but from his nefarious career even before the train robbery, perhaps he deserved it?

From his last days in prison, in between days on release in Evesham, he wrote to the press and the Welsh language version of the Liverpool Daily Echo printed his complaint that the nickname was 'a great embarrassment to his parents'. The plural there means he was either in contact still with his father later in life or, more likely, someone translating from English to Welsh to Scouse to English and uploading the results to a website to be read half a century later might have added an 's' by mistake. In other news that week, half the country was talking about strikes and the people had started to forget about the great train robbers.

I'm going to condense a full decade of Roy's life into these next few of paragraphs, as it covers his later stretch in various jails for the train robbery. There are the thoughts of four mundane walls, grey repetitive days and insufficient exercise. I was fortunate to get access to some letters he had sent from jail. There was the tiny bit of happiness of sending and receiving banal correspondence like the Christmas card sent to the Western Daily Press, with a picture of Brands Hatch racing circuit on the front and inside, in his distractive copper-plate handwriting, a message saying he was 'still running'. And there was the slapstick of Durham prison thinking they'd lost him, before doing a recount and admitting they hadn't. He was allowed one visitor for one thirty-minute visit a month and, because of his prison status, all his visitors were vetted by the Home Office. Upon later being downgraded from a category A (greatest risk) to category B, he complained as the facilities were better in category A prisons. They allowed him back.

The street he had grown up in, Doneraile Street in Fulham, was used for various scenes in an episode of The Professionals. In it, Bodie and Doyle pose as hitmen to infiltrate a mysterious group of assassins whose targets are all retired government officials. All very exciting. But there's little TV inside and Fulham was quietly going upmarket.

Some of his fellow robbers' belongings got auctioned off. He missed the funeral of Jim Clark (fellow racer from years back), which was attended by 'Name' and others. Biggs escaped in '65, first to Australia and then Brazil, where he essentially spent years flicking the vees and sunning himself, avoiding extradition due to getting a local girl pregnant. This escape cost him a quarter of all the money he had.

Biggs' caper earned the remaining robbers, such as Roy, eight months in solitary confinement in cells with no windows. The government were genuinely worried he'd escape, but he had no such intentions. He had a legal to and fro with the Press Complaints Commission about the media's use of 'The Weasel', saying it was 'causing acute embarrassment to his family', which was eventually thrown out on the basis that the police had said it so tough titty, Weasel-features. His favourite book in jail was Castrol Racing Drivers' Manual by Frank Gardner and Doug Nye. He had a stack of motorsport magazines and read every page, his favourite being Autosport. He shat in a bucket. I dunno. There are so few facts from this stretch in jail that you'll excuse me for the earthy guesswork. Probably absolutely nothing much happened, because that's sort of the point of jail.

His letters are a mix of banal, of hope and plans. He had plans of romance with the sister of a Formula One driver he was acquainted with, and mentions her in two letters, with talk of her being his shipmate and jokes about locking her in the brig. He had only had 'girlfriends' before, but was looking for a wife and thought she was the one (although it is apparent that she probably wasn't as enamoured as him). I have promised not to share names or details of this and, honestly, it feels like an intrusion even looking at his copper-plate handwriting from such a tough place. He comments on Formula One, mentioning the horror of Bandini's crash at Monaco, for example, but one thing that shines through is the desire to be accepted once he is out.

Roy regularly played football, particularly towards the end of his sentence. His first proper game was so boisterous that he couldn't sleep for three nights afterwards. He also took up gymnastics inside, coming a cropper and damaging a leg, but recovering to gain a certificate for his abilities. Keeping fit and staying out of trouble was his focus. I asked a prison worker friend what life was like inside in the '60s and '70s, hoping he'd get me a mooch around a nick for a taste of things. 'Have you seen Porridge?' he asked. 'It's just like that.' It's full of angry people, dangerous people, people plotting grand schemes, sad and lost people and some like Roy who just kept their head down for years on end.

Chapter 22 – '67, Buggy

In '67, the tedium was broken by the police. Roy was visited inside in connection with the murder of someone called John Buggy. Buggy was a gangster whose body had been found bound up with wire and full of bullet holes, floating in the sea off of Sussex. Once they'd worked out who the body was, they broke into his house and found a letter from Roy to Buggy, which then led them to ask Roy to explain a few things. Buggy was suspected of being the banker for the Great Train Robbery but, frankly, that's an accusation that could have been aimed at any of the very many people who had eagerly clawed at the mountain of cash the gang netted. I only see the letter connecting them, but the police clearly suspected something.

Buggy's body had been dumped from a rented speedboat called Shakespeare by men of 'Mediterranean' appearance and found by off-duty coppers who were fishing. 'Off-duty' might mean that they had been tipped off but didn't want to reveal their source or it could mean that they were off-duty. Buggy was an American living in London, confusingly known as 'Scotch Jack'. His girlfriend said he was a 'wonderfully kind man' and, perhaps in the same breath, confirmed he'd just done a 6-year stretch for shooting someone. Today, the sight of a small boat approaching a south-coast beach with foreign types aboard would have Farage frothing from the clifftops. Then, Roy said nothing and no one was charged with Buggy's death.

The earlier years of Roy's incarceration were a bit livelier. He had been in Durham nick, but then the Prison Service built a new, super-high-security jail on the Isle of Wight, called Parkhurst, and he and other high-risk prisoners were moved there in February '66. He was immediately given a hard time. Another prisoner had complained about something trivial and it quickly escalated into an 'us versus them' situation, with Roy on the wrong side to maintain his 'stay out of trouble' strategy for long. Prisoners barricaded themselves into their cells. The warders had a machine to break the hinges on the cells and gain access and, after some time, Roy's cell was opened and he supposedly received a beating. His books and papers were ripped up and a cream cake was stuffed into his record player.

His punishment was 15 days on bread and water. I had to double-check this. I couldn't believe that someone could be fed only bread and water for extended periods, but it seems that the practice was used until as late as '74. IRA member Michael Gaughan died on hunger strike in Parkhurst at this time. This isn't Porridge nor was it 'The Great St. Trinian's Train Robbery', which Roy would have been fortunate to miss, the last in a series featuring Frankie Howerd as 'Alphonse of Monte Carlo'. That ode to squealing camp nonsense marked a period of people in the media capitalising on the robbery. You can see where the kernel of the later plan to create their own, Nazi-flavoured, book comes from. The robbers were inside, often in solitary confinement or on bread and water rations, while the outside world profited from their story.

In October '65, Roy was moved from Leicester to Durham prison with a very twitchy governor worrying about escape. The Reading Evening Post (and others) reported that a suspicious looking Austin A40 with Grimsby registration plates had been hanging around the governor's house in Durham, helpfully printing his full address, which would have done wonders for the governor's peace of mind, no doubt. In '65, Peta Fordham published the first book about the Great Train Robbery. There's an original copy in The British Library. She was the daughter of one of the barristers on the case and privy to some juicy inside info. Still, the book was written in a careful, professional manner and the case was still fresh in many people's minds. Roy was properly miffed than someone could profit from his 'work' so soon. Others mentioned it. For example, the Bond film of '65, Thunderball, has a SPECTRE operative claiming to have received a consultation fee for the robbery and, in the same year, the Beatles released the film 'Help!' with a snide line from John Lennon '[the] Great Train Robbery, how's that going?'

On Amazon today, I can find 150 titles mentioning the Great Train Robbery, plus many films and TV series covering the same topic with subtitles like 'crime of the century', 'untold story', 'the curse', 'the 50th anniversary' and so on. I've ordered and read many books on the subject and, to be sure I didn't miss anything or have any money left at the end of the month, ordered multiple copies of some. I have not yet watched the 2013 BBC TV show about it, featuring Martin Compston playing Roy. Martin is an ex-football-playing Scotsman who lives in Las Vegas. It's another rehash of the same story. All this is another reason my book is about Roy, not the robbery, although I've had to sift through heaps of books regurgitating the same facts about it, including some with 'facts' that I accidentally created myself years ago.

Soon after his conviction, Brian Field (later known as Brian Carlton, remember) appealed and had his sentence cut. His role in the Great Train Robbery had been an administrative one, and the only practical job he was tasked with was bodged. He was to pay a man called Mark to burn down the farm and had assured the rest of the gang it had been done on time. The gang (Roy included) didn't believe Brian and had called him to a meeting. Once his mistake was revealed, some of the gang wanted to kill him on the spot, but Brian talked his way out.

Soon after his early release in '67, Brian was caught by Scotch Jack Buggy, who assumed he was sitting on some of the proceeds from the Great Train Robbery, and tortured him. There may have also been a revenge motive from members of the gang instructing Buggy. Field immediately changed his name, moved house and very effectively vanished from the public eye. Reinventing himself as Brian Carlton, he married a younger woman, successfully got into the publishing business, made friends with Prince Felipe of Spain and bought a shiny new Porsche.

Following some email ping-pong, phone calls and quite a few letters, I now had the details of two interesting women who had visited him in jail early in his sentence. One replied quickly and was quite happy to chat anonymously; we'll call her B. The other is Valerie Pirie, secretary to Sir Stirling Moss MBE and a very well-connected lady. She's mother to Mia Forbes Pirie, who we met earlier. Some say that Roy had once raced against, and beaten, Moss. Val Pirie is nicknamed 'Viper', only partially, I suspect, because of wordplay. I called her and was told, rather abruptly, 'I'm on my way to Lerwick!' She explained that a flight to the Shetland Islands town was so expensive that it was cheaper to take a boat there. 'And then you get the bonus of five days on a boat!' she exclaimed, batting off my concerns about the six hours of daylight and famously inclement North Sea weather at this time of year. Lerwick being further north than Saint Petersburg and most of the Scandinavian capitals is a fact that I did not dare share with her. Val is very fond of Roy, she made that clear, and we agreed to meet again if/when she ever gets back from Lerwick.

Val had been a director of a business named after her former employer and Moss himself was a bugger for shamelessly endorsing allsorts. He leant his name to the rather ordinary Audi 80, the Australian Chrysler Valiant, a 360cc Suzuki kei car and a freaky little Mini-based thing called the TiCi ('titchy'), which can't have been any worse than Schumacher lending his name to a special edition of the Fiat Seicento, I suppose. Moss was one of the first drivers to capitalise on his name as a brand.

I had a nice message from a property manager in Chelsea. As Roy and others were into their first years of incarceration, a caretaker at Nell Gwynne House in Chelsea opened a service hatch at a top-floor flat to remove a bag of litter. It was a wooden hatch, with a 'Jack and Jill' arrangement to a hatch on the inside of the apartment, allowing the inhabitant to leave their rubbish for collection without going outside. An envelope dropped into the caretaker's hands with a set of plans outlining the Great Train Robbery. It had been sellotaped to the inside of this hatch some time ago, and although the police had raided the apartment when the gang were arrested, they never found these plans. The surprised caretaker passed them to the authorities, though the gang was already locked up. The gang had been using this flat for meetings, as Roy had taken it on a short-term lease.

Chapter 23 – '60s, Skip Barber's pit stop

Val described herself as Moss's girl Friday and had published a book about him and, if my sleuthing was right, was living in a handsome house up the posh end of London. Having wasted £2.50 on stamps chasing Bernie, she got a 2nd class letter and my email address to respond to. Looking at how she'd capitalised on her career with Moss (she'd even sold the film rights to her life, I think), I somehow doubted she'd spill the beans without wanting something out of it. That might sound uncharitable, and of course she's under no obligation to help me with my work, but I had added her name to that of Bernie's of people unlikely to want to get involved in my weaselly caper before eating humble pie when she called me en route to Lerwick.

I asked Val where she first met Roy and she explained that a celebrity fixer called Malcolm Hall, who worked for one of the TV companies, contacted her and said that Roy would like a chat about racing. It's very clear that Val has always been very well connected. She name-drops Sir James Scott Douglas, who spent two sizeable inheritances, left the family estate in ruins and (possibly) ate himself to death. I don't know why she mentioned him, but she seemed to assume that I knew who he was. I now do. Malcolm Hall was a friend of Roy's, because Roy probably liked to keep track of some celebrities in order to burgle them. Roy turned up at Mallory when she was there, with Gordon Goodie, who scared her. An 'ugly man', she said.

Val enthuses about Roy, saying he just liked racing and 'he was a very honest person'. I interrupt her to gently ask about the police reportedly disarming Roy during the shooting to be told 'bollocks!' and, later, 'bloody police!' She said that the gang knew about the shooting before the police did, to which I suggested that it points to a premeditated crime, which antagonises Val further. I don't blame her. She's clearly very fond of Roy and her 85 years have not blunted her opinions. I feel I am getting on her tits a bit, albeit unintentionally.

Val softens and laughs at some of her memories, explaining that Roy once stole the personal car of a Flying Squad officer, from straight outside the station, to commit a robbery. He returned it to the same spot after the crime. The red tops were chasing her and many others for information on Roy. Of course, they said nothing. Nick Syrett of the BRSCC kept reporters waiting, laconically telling them he wanted to watch the end of the cricket first, before informing them to bugger off. But Roy made a friend in photographer Norman Potter, who he allowed to photograph him in return for Norman paying Roy his fees when Roy was short. The press, the police and the criminal underworld were all somehow entwined. Today we like life in black or white, good or bad, but Roy's life illustrates a time of blurred lines.

Val asks about some of Roy's other capers, things that perhaps she had not heard. We laughed at some of his stunts together. I made the mistake of telling her about the wedding and mentioned some guests that had been invited – 'but why not me?!' she exclaimed. I told her that, if it was of any comfort, I hadn't been invited either. Roy and Anthea's wedding was 40 years ago. I asked (as I wasn't sure myself) if she knew where the wedding had been held. She then made a noise that sounded like what children make to mimic a passing Formula One car. A sort of 'nyeeeeoooo' sound. I asked her to spell it. 'E W E L L', she said in Times New Roman. 'Eeee-well?' I countered. She doesn't suffer fools (like me) gladly. 'No! Nyeeeeooo!' she shouted, 'Nyeeeeooo! Nyeeeeooo!', sounding like a passing Grand Prix. Apparently, having checked with my missus who is from down that way, it's pronounced something like 'yule'. Sorry Val. She said she didn't understand the shooting, and that Roy lived two lives. We wrap up.

B, on the other hand, told a story of making a prison visit and being made to sit in a cold, miserable waiting room with a 'load of rough, common types' for ages, before seeing Roy. She had never even met him before, his charisma and reputation appealing to her, perhaps. Another female admirer came, someone who I have been asked not to name, someone semi-famous who I will call X. Roy fell head over heels for her and proposed, getting someone to buy her a large diamond engagement ring. Perhaps only then the realisation of waiting a decade or more for her man dawned, and she went cold.

Early in his incarceration, Roy was sent cyanide by a friend. This might have been an honest offer to give him a way out of the 30-year sentence he had just started, or it might have been a warning against grassing up others who remained at large. Another of the train robbers had paid some thugs to hide his girlfriend and baby from the authorities, then paid them again to hide the baby separately from the mother as 'that is safer', then again to release the baby, who was essentially being held hostage from its poor mother, who was going out of her mind with worry.

Roy barely knew who to trust, other than his mother, Violet. 'The Great Train Robbers should have been shot', said the Chief Constable of Durham Constabulary, leaving everyone wondering that, if this is what the 'good guys' say, then what would those crooks considering themselves wronged by the gang do. 'Violent criminals should be quietly disposed of', concluded the Chief Constable, Alec Muir. Muir had been christened 'Alec in Blunderland' for some professional mistakes. He blustered on about criminals 'attacking the jail with tanks and nuclear weapons'. No wonder the prison governor was twitchy.

Roy spent more than a third of his adult life in jail. As his racing contemporaries lapped and lapped, he was stuck in the pits. If his life was a Formula One race, then he was a driver called Skip Barber.

Skip holds the dubious record of having completed a race having spent a third of it stuck in the pit lane. This happened when Roy was in jail, unsurprisingly. At the '72 Canadian Grand Prix, Skip made a single pit stop, found a problem with the throttle of his March and spent over an hour frantically trying to get the car to work properly, before finally joining the race a full 56 laps behind everyone else. The race was won by Jackie Stewart, Peter Revson was second, Denny 'doesn't poo in the woods' Hulme came third and Roy's old sparring partner Graham Hill was eighth.

I'd like to mention that Derek Bell came last, and the reason for shoe-horning that otherwise meaningless bit of information in is to boost my own racing credentials by sharing that Bell once looked at me and snorted 'I'm not getting in a car with *him*!' Yeah, I'm famous. Skip spent a third of his race in the pits and Roy spent a third of his adult life in clink.

Skip had the unconventional notion that, to be a first-class racing driver, all anyone needed was tuition and that he was the man that could, er, tuit. He opened a driver school and, to his credit, made a decent fist of it before retiring. Depending on if you're reading this book at the time of publication, all fresh pages and clean cover, then he's alive and well aged 87 (as would Roy had been, coincidentally). Or if this book represents to you a musty old 50p car boot purchase some years later, then Skip's probably croaked it, and anyway – why didn't you buy this new so I could have my 25p royalty, you cheapskate?!

There's no doubt that driver training can help, but there's a strong argument that says you are born with talent. People like Graham Hill, for example, only got into driving late in life, and he was a born winner. Senna had it from birth. The Nigel had it. Conversely, Luca Badoer did a record 2,364 laps in Formula One but huge experience and world-class training never netted him a single point, despite even driving for Ferrari at one point. He did, however, get fined for repeatedly speeding in the pit lane. I think you're born with it. I think Roy was born with it. He just wasted it.

Chapter 24 – '60s, Burlington Arcade

Others who visited Roy during those early months in jail included his old mechanic, Bobby Pelham, Nick Syrett, director of the BRSCC, and Val Pirie. There was a startling piece of analysis from someone who I presumed had visited him, but hadn't – Dr Mia Kellmer Pringle. Dr Mia said at the time that the great train robbers were bright children who simply didn't make the grade. I'm grateful for any contemporary psychological insights into Roy and his band of baddies, but this guesswork from a distance isn't telling us much, is it, Dr Mia? Her words made the papers anyway. My notes are very scruffy, and this is intentional.

Years ago, in my day job, I went to a really, really boring meeting with a new notepad and my only notes during the whole day's meeting was the one single line, in capital letters, 'I AM BORED SHITLESS'. I forgot my notepad and the person I met kindly posted it back to me with a Post-it note on the cover saying 'Richard, you forgot this, it was nice to meet you. I hope the meeting wasn't too boring for you.' Since then, I write in a kind of mad scrawl, sometimes in German or Norwegian, just in case I write something that I don't want others to read. The problem with this technique is that I often cannot decipher my own notes.

My notes from meeting Brodie had something about a Dr Msomethingsomethingnotsure who he'd had a legal spat with, and I wondered if this was the same doctor. I messaged him. No, said Brodie, Roy's dodgy doctor girlfriend was Dr Mary, not Dr Mia. He said Dr Mary had a friend and they all went skiing as a foursome once. Fearful of another £220 book buy, I did not question this. I dug further. Mary is actually Maryann and was quite an explosive character.

I need to jump to the '70s now, when Roy and Maryann were with friends. They were doing a crossword and he was feeling mischievous. 'Here's a clue for you', said Roy. 'The postman lost the mail.' Maryann looked up and asked 'how many letters?' Roy replied 'the whole f*cking lot.' Roy laughed but she tried to throttle him, very angry. Later, Roy bugged her office and found that she was having an affair, then rammed her lover's car with his pickup truck. Maryann and Roy had a financial spat, which, I believe, was one of the causes of him trying to remortgage the family house when his father-in-law was shot. I digress, let's get back to jail.

Roy's first cell was number A2/29 at Leicester jail. There had only ever been one escape from Leicester jail when Roy was locked up (and there have been none since); safe-breaker Albert Hattersley, who, despite suffering a broken ankle, managed to go on the 'run' for several hours before recapture.

Inconveniently for the wobbly timeline in this book, and contrary to anecdotal 'information', Roy did *not* rob London's Burlington Arcade in '64. I really, really wanted him to have done this one. The style of the robbery, the targets, the getaway car, it had every hallmark of a Weasel job. Roy was in jail at the time and no amount of date reassessment would make it fit. The Arcade was definitely robbed in June of that year and Roy was definitely under lock and key. Some people are convinced Roy did it.

In a crime that was never solved, six heavies squeezed into a Jaguar Mark X and drove down the very narrow Arcade, smashing windows and grabbing valuables from window displays as they went. The timid shopworkers threw a plant pot at the car as it passed, but otherwise the robbers were unimpeded and drove off like The Nigel. Soon afterwards, the Arcade's owners installed bollards at either end to prevent anyone else attempting it.

The Arcade has always had its own police force, predating the actual police force in London by a few years. At first, they were recruited from the Earl of Burlington's cavalry regiment and later, when they got an upgrade from horse to tank, they employed ex-tankies, before finally running out of suitable applicants and hiring an ex-RAF dog handler. They used to have a comfortable armchair on which to rest while on duty, placed discretely near the entrance. The gang got away with £35,000 of jewellery, without Roy's input.

What he probably did do, however, is a very similar smash and grab at four jewellers' shops burgled overnight in the early hours of 14th October 1959 in the very same spot. On that occasion, the gang apparently got away with a staggering £210,000. I'll guess that the shop owners' insurance claims covered everything of value they had stolen, plus everything had not had been stolen but could conjure up some paperwork for. And this well-insured location is seemingly jinxed. One end got bombed in the war and in '36, it mysteriously caught fire and was immediately looted.

Today, what is Britain's first ever shopping centre is owned by the Reuben brothers who are worth £24 billion thanks in no small part to dealing in Russian state assets. The pair make extensive use of offshore tax havens, said The Times, and are probably insured to the hilt for when the next robbery takes place, said me. There are seven guards in total nowadays, including (recently) an Albanian and an Afghan – all comfy chairs have been removed.

Chapter 25 – '64, The Movie Scene

On 1st November 1964, Roy was found guilty of The Great Train Robbery and sentenced to 30 years in prison. He had hired a QC to defend him. Roy's defence largely hinged on the witness statement of a taxi driver called Derek Brown, who stated that he had been with Roy for some hours around the time of the crime. The QC also pointed out that the item found with Roy's fingerprints on it, at Leatherslade Farm where the gang hid, could have been placed before or after the robbery and did not link Roy directly to the robbery. Some later said that his fingerprints were found on a Monopoly board, others on a cup and saucer (Roy often used a proper cup and saucer) or on a dish used to feed milk to the farm cat. But the evidence used was a salt shaker. The court also heard that his fingerprints had been found on an American magazine called 'The Movie Scene'. He had a thing about actors being rich wasters and, therefore, fair game. Roy knew he'd taken off his gloves at various points during the handling of things at the farm, and also knew he was in big trouble.

As anyone who has read any of the many books on the robbery, Nazi-themed or otherwise, will know, Brian Field (the gang's solicitor friend) was supposed to arrange the burning down of the farm once they'd left to destroy evidence. But he didn't, which left fingerprints, paint samples and other things that eventually lead to convictions – Roy's included. The taxi driver was a stooge, of course, and no one believed that Roy would have invited a cabbie back to his flat in Chelsea just for a chat into the evening.

The gang had committed the crime with little or no thought as to what they should do afterwards. It was simply a way bigger heist than any of them had ever done before. The farm was their downfall. They could easily have scarpered straight back to London with the loot before the police woke up, but there was suspicion within the gang, and a lack of trust, so they decided to divvy up the loot before scarpering, and a local farm was the best place for that. Roy didn't trust Ronnie Biggs, in particular.

In Roy's defence, Ron Tauranac was called. Ron was one of the founders of Brabham, a leading race-car manufacturer, the sort that got stolen many pages ago in New Zealand. Ron was a kind, industrious and rather shy man who was called up as a character witness for Roy. He described Roy as a 'meteoric driver' and got confused as to who he should address, and how, because in court everyone was wearing suits and looked the same to him. He knew him as a customer, although he did not regularly deal with all customers himself. I don't think Ron really knew what kind of a person Roy was, away from racing. Stirling Moss was repeatedly asked to be a character reference, but refused. He was on a sticky wicket. It is said that the average legal bill for each of the gang members was in the region of £30k. For comparison, an office manager might earn £1,500 a year at the time. Many of the lawyers treated themselves to flash new cars and suits, getting rich from inflated fees, all paid for by money stolen by the gang, money that ultimately belonged to someone else.

With people at work no longer believing that Teams glitches were really preventing me from doing my day job, I was called to London for a meeting without biscuits, with the subject line of the invitation being 'achievements'. A train ride to London with my laptop and a spare coat gave me the opportunity to explore where Roy had been caught on 10th December 1963. I deliberately chose the third carriage from the front of the train to travel on. The train robbers knew that the money was always carried in the third carriage. I chose not to train surf this time. At work, I cheerily said hello to anyone I saw, draped my spare coat over the back of a chair, left my oft-dropped laptop switched on, then snuck out the back for a trip to St John's Wood. St John's Wood is handily served by a tube station of the same name, but in my haste to get there and back before my absence was noticed, I got off one stop too early and walked from Baker Street instead.

My ultimate destination was 14 Ryder's Terrace, St John's Wood. Miles away, uphill, past the cricket ground. My sweaty power walk took me past the famous Abbey Road Studios and I managed to completely miss both this and the iconic pedestrian crossing outside. I later googled to see if I'd missed anything actually worth seeing and was reassured by someone saying you're not allowed inside anyway, and 'Konameme' commenting on the outside thus: 'i tried to re-enact the Beatles cover and i got run over. i later died in the hospital'.

Ryder's Terrace is a short stretch of mews houses, round the back of a row of shops. There's a narrow lane in, then a kind of T-junction with a short stretch of houses and dead ends. One dead end has a low brick wall, which someone fitter and nosier than me could probably climb over pretty easily and land in the extensive gardens of a fancy house. Leading off this sort of cul-de-sac is a narrow pedestrian path back to the main road.

It's a good spot to hide. There is only really one main way in, but, depending on your interpretation of trespass laws, four ways out. And it's surprisingly quiet. Only my gentle panting, which caused a worried lady walking her dog to walk a little quicker, and someone unhelpfully opening their front door when I wanted to take a photo of the street but not want to get anyone in shot who might not want to be in shot. And I certainly wasn't going to explain what I was doing there when I should have been miles away talking about achievements and strategy and things.

Roy's house, number 14, had sold not too long ago for over £1 million, with the agent mentioning the robbery. Roy had had a friend rent it for him, on a nine-month lease, this 'tall, dark' friend had been spotted by neighbours but little had been seen of Roy. A blonde lady was in there with him, occasionally grabbing a pint of milk from the doorstep, but otherwise keeping themselves to themselves. But parked nearby was Roy's Jaguar E-Type (one of the first made) and a Mini, clues that something was afoot here.

Nearby streets today have white Range Rovers with huge wheels ground against kerbs, people talking so loudly on their car phone that I can hear disjointed snippets of conversation as they drift by, orange-faced young women and people walking with their faces in phones, clutching coffee, looking into another world instead of appreciating the one under their nose. It is nice around here; look up! I send a note to the inhabitant of Roy's house and wonder if I'll get a response. What kind of person lives here now?

Back to number 14 and Roy's arrest; it's likely that the blonde hiding with him was Patricia Willey, a policewoman. There was a very unusual article in the press during Roy's trial about her. She had been on the Great Train Robbery case in some capacity and based at Harrow Road Police Station, but had decided that, after 7 years' service, she was leaving the police to join the Cunard shipping line and work overseas. And then tell the newspapers. And the newspapers decided that this was newsworthy. I believe this was a ruse to throw someone off her scent. At the time, Scotland Yard used 'decoy girls' and this might have been done to hide her from possible repercussions. Roy was, according to one of the officers on the case, 'the most intelligent of all the train robbers'.

Chapter 26 – '64, Sheffield Telegraph

Around the same time as Roy was in custody, his old mate Bobby Pelham was charged with handling stolen money. The money was deposited with Bobby as payment for some parts for Roy's Brabham, but it was more than the police thought was reasonable, and he was nicked. It was payment for some parts, plus a final 'thank you' from Roy. While Bobby was talking to the police and the robbers were in custody, someone cut the brake lines on his family car, and when he took his family on an outing, they were very lucky to escape serious injury when the brakes failed. Roy couldn't have done this, and I don't think he would have instructed others to do it either, but it was definitely a warning from someone to keep quiet as the trial rumbled on.

Pelham was convicted and when he had served his time, he changed his name and moved away with his family. Roy was later quite upset about this. They had been friends for some time, although Pelham was a friend from the racing world who, like most others in the racing world, wanted no part of the crime scene that Roy came from. Pelham (under a different name) died much later, far from London, with Roy placing a short obituary to him in the local newspaper. Being around train robbers was dangerous.

In March '64, the Sheffield Telegraph Trophy, a trophy awarded annually, was anonymously returned to Cadwell Park race circuit. Roy had won it before and, knowing he was going to jail, safely returned it, as he wouldn't be able to defend it the following year. He never wanted to leave a bad impression in the racing world.

He also received a visit from a girl called Michelle, who had asked her mum to write a letter to the Queen demanding better conditions for Roy. 'There's no romance between us', she said at the time, and confirmed to me in person when I tracked her down quite recently, which probably freaked her out a bit. There's a report in the Scotsman that hints she might have been his fiancée, even though they only met once, in jail. I think she's a bit embarrassed about this, which would have Theroux leaving awkward silences for people to fill, but that's not my style. I think the embarrassment itself says something. I move on.

Roy had 73 visits in total, some from hangers-on, others from worried family members of the gang, his mother and others. One visitor's name stood out to me; Tom Driberg. Driberg was a very peculiar chap, a friend of the Krays and other criminals. He asked in the House of Commons about the restricted visiting rights of train robbery prisoners, for reasons no one can explain. Driberg was an ex-newspaper columnist, suspected communist and an outgoing, unapologetic homosexual at a time when it was still illegal. Some years before he visited Roy in jail, Winston Churchill described him as 'the sort of person who gives sodomy a bad name'. Who knows what Driberg wanted with jail visits.

I dashed back to the office from my quick visit to Roy's lair, then faked interest in a job less interesting than stalking some dead racing driver. When Roy was captured, he was carrying £12,000 in a holdall. That's the equivalent, in today's money, of a third of a million pounds. Police knocked on the door in Ryder's Terrace and asked him to open up, to which he replied, 'what, so I can get nicked?!'

A Deirdre Holloway looks delighted at getting her face in the Daily Express. She lived opposite and spilled the gossip to reporter Russell McPhedran. McPhedran later photographed the terrorist attack at the Munich Olympics in '72, the Profumo affair and Princess Anne. Just for the avoidance of doubt, those were three completely separate incidents. He also blagged entry to the '20 years of freedom party' held by Ronnie Biggs in Brazil in '85 by giving him posters of photographs he'd taken. This allowed him to get further pictures from this notorious party. His obituary says that he was a man of great integrity, and I admire his sleuthing.

Neighbours reported seeing Roy climb out of a skylight, shin down a drainpipe and then jump over a garden wall before being caught by a strapping copper called Steve Moore. The same wall that I had leaned against earlier and got muck on my trousers, which made my outfit look way more bohemian than the others at work, who wondered where I'd been in the building all day. 'Meetings', I told them. Which is sort of true.

I later got a very friendly email from Dilan Abeya, resident today of number 14. He's clearly a talented chap, speaking Japanese, doing things with AI and (says his profile on Google) is 'credited as the UK's top model and financial personality by Entrepreneur and Forbes'. There's a copy of the newspaper report of the time of the arrest on Dilan's wall. You can do your own punchline about investment banking and the biggest robbery in British history here, if you like. He asked me to include a web link to his website, but clicks don't work well in print. Sorry Dilan.

Chapter 27 – '63, The Mountain

Time on the run, knowing that he'd be caught anyway, must have been lively for Roy in '63. There is a famous television clip, which you might find on YouTube, of Roy winning that Sheffield Telegraph Trophy very soon after the train robbery when it was sort of an open secret that he'd been involved, but the police were a few too many steps behind him. It was recorded at Cadwell Park in Lincolnshire, barely two weeks after the robbery, and the commentator, David Roscoe, jovially remarks 'that's the last we'll see of that trophy!' Roy looks sheepish. George Duncan was the producer and kindly shared the background of that memorable moment with me and original footage. Many people suspected Roy.

At the same time, he had sent his entry papers to a Formula Junior race at Brands Hatch for September of that year. He might have expected to be caught, but wanted to dream that he could continue as normal, and perhaps just grab one last race, before he eventually had his collar felt in December '63. He used a fake address for his race application at Brands Hatch; Flat 456b Alexandra Road, Harrow. This was a flat above shops next to a cinema and is now a flat above a hairdressers next to the Zoroastrian Centre, which recently held a webinar on the menopause.

In August, he was due to race at Kirkistown in Northern Ireland. The organiser knew Roy and commented that he was a 'small, very pleasant, polite and well-dressed man. Took his racing seriously enough and was certainly no playboy'. But Roy didn't show up.

In September '63, the police distributed 50,000 'wanted' posters in the UK, plus 500 in Europe. Around the same date, Roy went to Goodwood to practice for a race but scarpered early, towing his Brabham on a bouncing trailer behind his powerful Jaguar, when someone tipped him off that the police were coming for him.

Earlier in this book I mentioned Peter Procter, the man who read a eulogy at Roy's funeral, and a name I vaguely knew from motorsport somewhere but couldn't remember why. He had an almost lifelong friendship with Roy and, thanks partially to that slightly unusual spelling of his surname, a hunch led me to an address in the Yorkshire Dales. One letter later and I got a phone call from one of the nicest people I have met in a very, very long time.

When Brodie was in hospital after a very hefty crash, he wrote to Roy in jail, as 'there's always someone worse off than you' and they struck up a friendship. Similarly, Peter and Roy's friendship came when Roy wrote to Peter in hospital, where he was recovering from a crash which left him with 65% burns. Roy posted a jolly, rainbow-coloured card, wishing Peter a speedy recovery. I don't like to mention this, frankly, as this accident should not define who Peter is as a person, but I now recall seeing his picture advertising Les Leston flame-retardant racewear in old issues of Motor Sport magazine. And now he welcomes me into his beautiful house telling me not to worry about taking my boots off 'as long as that's Yorkshire mud on them'.

I did not expect, when I started writing this book, that I would come across such interesting people. Meeting Peter and his wife Shirley was something I will never forget. Peter was a builder in Barnsley who, through brains and hard graft, ended up buying a 1954 Aston Martin. He was also a professional cyclist, winning 'King of the Mountain' in '51, which could easily be an epithet for the man himself. He, Bob Mallard and Gordon Thomas were the top three cyclists of their era and yet were overlooked for national representation for reasons you'll find in his book, 'Pedals and Pistons'. As he grew disillusioned with the politics of British cycling, he was invited to an event at Oulton Park with the Aston Martin Owners Club and became hooked on motorsport. Shirley is also in her '90s (you'd never tell) and is great fun. Peter teasingly called her 'champ chaser'. They've been married over 70 years and have five sons.

One of Peter's early races in Formula Junior was the same race weekend in '63 that Roy prematurely left. In practice, Peter and fellow drivers were slipstreaming in order to gain an advantage, when Roy came charging through the field, almost wiping everyone out. Peter stomped down the paddock to have a word with the 'bloody idiot' Roy, who told him 'So what? If I crash, I crash.' Peter said the young Londoner was 'a damned nuisance'. Roy then scarpered from Goodwood and, as we know, was eventually arrested. Peter was driving for Ken Tyrrell at the time and the two of them were driving to the circuit on race day and were gobsmacked to see Roy 'The Weasel' James' face on the front page of the papers. He was a wanted man. Peter's accident was 3 years later, at the same circuit, when his car was hit from behind and burst into flames. He was lucky to survive.

In '66, when Peter was recuperating, Roy sent his friendly card and the two struck up a friendship. Roy's letters were sent on prison-stamped papers. Peter's replies were typed as his hands were so damaged. Peter later competed in the Monte Carlo Rally and even competed in the Le Mans Classic in 2002, when he was 72. I am totally humbled by his achievements and his modesty. He only quit cycling recently (he's 94 at the time of writing) due to 'a bit of lung cancer', is recovering from a heart attack and yet is clearly fitter and sharper than me. I'm young enough to be his grandson (but am not, says Ancestry.com). His memory is so sharp and he still drives down to Portugal to holiday and is involved with the BRDC and other charitable groups. He was surprised, and pleased, when I told him that his picture is on the wall of the local pub.

I read through his correspondence with Roy. Roy mentions a visit from 'Mick', who I take to be his old mate Micky Ball (who Peter did not know), and Rod and Birgitte, which must be Formula Junior racer Rodney Banting and a friend. Roy complains about the attention of the guards and hints at the rough and tumble of prison life, but seems consigned to his fate. There's an eloquence in his writing, and it's always hopeful, even in those early years. There's the odd unrepeatable phrase that might offend sensitive modern ears, but, remember, these are the words of someone born in '35. Peter still has Roy's toolbox, with his silversmith tools, and is keen to return them to Samantha, Roy's daughter. But, like me, he's unable to track her down. They might get auctioned off for charity.

We talked about Trevor Taylor and Stirling Moss and Shirley joked about 'sleeping with' Jimmy Clark (they both fell asleep in the back of Peter's car on a long drive once). Stirling Moss' charming habit of calling everyone 'old boy' was a ruse to hide his inability to remember people's names, said Peter. Peter built a bowling alley and got Jimmy Clark to open it. They were good friends. Clark, you may know, holds the record for the greatest gap between first and second place in a Formula One race. He won the '63 Belgian Grand Prix a full five minutes ahead of the second-placed car. Shirley was also full of beans and told us about The Doghouse Owners' Club that I'd written to earlier. Both of them were so fond of Roy. His mother, Violet, had stayed with them, as had Roy's sister Joanna (who emigrated to New Zealand many years ago and vanished off the radar). Roy's 'wild' kids, who kept their dad on his toes, had also stayed there.

The Roy they describe seems incapable of the crimes he committed. They did not gloss over his failings, but loved spending time with him and pointed out his positive qualities. He was very funny, liked a joke and was keen to be accepted by the motorsport fraternity. Peter wrote to Roy, in jail, to build his hope in the future. He offers to manage Roy and assures him that the world of racing would love to have him back. It's a sign of great friendship between them. But it also highlights Roy's need to be accepted in a different world from the one he came from. Peter painted a picture of drivers, mechanics, fans and friends, all mixing and enjoying life. As Peter talked of racing a Lotus in Formula 2, he showed me pictures and trophies from a magical time in motorsport and it left me itching to get behind the wheel myself.

To follow in Roy's footsteps, I went to first to Cadwell Park in Lincolnshire, a hilly circuit in a flat county. Being a man of modest finances, I shared an old Volkswagen Golf with a mate, paid to join a weekend trackday and hoovered the cobwebs out of my Deliveroo helmet. Cadwell was established as a sporting venue in '34 by Mr Mansfield Wilkinson of Louth, if you're interested. Around the time of Roy's appearance there, the circuit had just been lengthened to 2.1 miles, as part of a plan to attract Formula 3 racing. A lap record for single seaters on the full circuit was set in a Formula Libre car that same summer of '63 in a Lotus 22 – a record which stood for 20 years. The Lotus 22 had 100 horsepower and went round in 1 minute 44 seconds. It's the kind of time Roy would have set. The Golf has nearly twice the power.

You're not really supposed to time laps on trackdays, it's a safety thing to discourage racing, but I can't just come here and drive round in a circle looking for brunch. I liked the idea of trying to match the kind of time Roy was doing, my superior power compensating for my near-total lack of racing experience, making it a sort of fair fight. In order to time my progress but not break any rules, I decided to take advantage of the car stereo and some useful music. Rifling through the back catalogue of Screeching Weasel, I found a song of 1 minute and 50 seconds duration called 'I Hate Your Guts on Sunday' on an album called 'How to Make Enemies and Irritate People'. The name of the band, the song length and the song title all seemed entirely appropriate.

There's a section of Cadwell called the Mountain, which seems a rather grand title for what is essentially a bit of a steep hill until you stand and watch cars getting airborne at this point. But not my car. I had a procession behind me. I desperately wanted to get the car in the air but I only succeeded in making myself feel extremely nauseous as the old Golf made horrible slurring sounds when the front wheels went light. And it smelled bad, a mechanical fug that filled the cabin.

The music might have been well matched but it was completely absolutely bloody terrible. The singer has all the aural appeal of a gobby American teenager having a temper tantrum while someone beats him in the goolies with a banjo. A Google reviewer calls it 'purile, moronic', which would also be a pretty accurate description of my attempt to match Roy's lap times in a Volkswagen Golf. I did not fare any better at Goodwood. I did one lap in an Alfa Romeo with no brakes with my girlfriend screaming constantly and, later in the paddock, under his breath, Noel Edmonds called me a twat. A photographer shared with me a photograph which clearly shows one of my rear wheels sort of hanging off the car. I thought it felt funny but it's an Alfa Romeo so I forgave it.

Chapter 28 – '63, Two nuns

The police hunt for Roy was extensive and, thanks to the posters, there were many false sightings. He was seen in a white Wolseley car, driving with a blonde lady in Tipperary, Ireland. I know what you're thinking, you're thinking that's a long way to go. Sorry. He was also seen dressed as a vicar in a 'rural district'. I like the idea of pumped-up Bobbies jumping on every single slim, dark-haired, 5'4" male priest they saw, as that's basically all of them, isn't it?

There was a report that a garage in Battersea where Roy had once kept a car received a message for him from a woman called Lillian cryptically saying 'Roy, I'm going to Vienna'. Closer to home, and more plausibly, he was seen in an area of Chelsea called World's End. This is probably true, and perhaps someone got their sighting date mixed up, because, at the time of the robbery, Roy did live in a flat in Chelsea. Mischievous kids at a summer fete in the West Country made a sign saying 'Catch me if you can, The Weasel'. Then someone rang the police, claiming to be the *other* Weasel, complaining that Roy James shouldn't be called the Weasel at all.

This keystone cops stuff didn't abate for months. In September, a train ticket seller in Italy claims to have sold Roy and another gang member two tickets to Venice, and the Mirror reckoned he was in South America, and, clutching at straws even more, that he had bow legs. He was in Sudbury, Suffolk, and driving a blue Ford Consul in Bexley with a poodle on the passenger seat. The police were inundated. Tommy Butler, the lead policeman on the case, was arrested when looking for one of the gang on a beach in the south of France, the Sûreté Nationale mistaking him for a peeping Tom.

Fellow robbers Bruce Reynolds and John Daly, together with Roy, were reported as having had a pub meal together in the Fountain Inn near Kidderminster. They ordered huge quantities of food, ate and drank greedily, covered their faces with their hands when the bill came and paid with large-denomination notes. This all sounds so utterly implausible that I reckon the pub themselves concocted this story in order to welcome a swarm of eager visitors for a crime case that was all over the media, everywhere. This story appeared on the front pages of many newspapers and was probably a stroke of cheeky marketing genius by the landlord. The police said 'we hope the public keep reporting sightings' while probably clocking up lots of juicy overtime and having a jolly good laugh at all the cranks calling in.

I spoke to a police call handler about the kind of rubbish they have to deal with. Overshadowing the genuine and often bloody awful calls they handle, there's a stream of people complaining that the police have 'upset their dog' or asking 'there's a cost of living crisis – 'ow can you afford the petrol for your 'elecopter?' and similar madness. Someone once called Leicestershire Police to simply utter the word 'filth', before hanging up.

In fact, Roy had spent some time hiding at Bobby Pelham's house in Lonsdale Road, Notting Hill, and was later hiding in St John's Wood. He had paid a friend at Battersea Power Station to burn the clothes he'd worn at the robbery. Police pulled apart his Brabham and Mini, looking for clues. 'They will be searched nut and bolt', said coppers, who probably had a great time ripping apart two nice cars that played absolutely no part in anything. His Jaguar E-Type (taken from Ryder's Terrace) was sold, and restored in recent years.

The train robbery furore raged on. He had checked into a hotel in Hitchin as Mr James of Coventry (clever double bluff using his own name or idiot receptionist – you decide), before leaving without paying his bill. He'd also been seen checking into a hotel in Jersey, boarding a ferry to Ireland and was possibly dressed as a priest. Some of this added up to give police in Northern Ireland cause to mistakenly stop and search two nuns. A friend of Roy's told me that he initially stayed for some time with a bookmaker in Putney, but got fed up of hanging around the house all day and had to move out when the bookie's bored wife started coming on to him.

Roy grew a beard, moved to St. John's Wood and walked around Regent's Park at night to keep fit and stay sane. Straight after the robbery, when he was moving huge amounts of cash about, he and fellow robber Charlie Wilson were in a Mini in East London when news of the robbery came on the radio with the information that their farm hideout had been found (and, therefore, it hadn't been burned down as planned). Roy simply said 'That's it, then. We're nicked.'

Chapter 29 – '63, Lion tamer or astronaut or something

Roy was at large for just four months after the robbery. There's much talk about how 'meticulously planned' the robbery was and how their only mistake was the inability of their gang to burn the evidence at the farm. In later life, Roy said they'd simply gone too big. They could have robbed a couple of smaller trains, or taken a smaller amount, and not suffered the avalanche of attention that the biggest robbery in British history actually created. There is no way they would have ever gotten away with it for long. It's impossible. The sheer volume of cash flooding into the criminal market would have led to someone grassing, someone making a mistake, someone showing off etc. Little honour amongst thieves and all that, although Brodie reckons Roy would never lie to anyone, ever.

The police were chasing lots of legitimate leads, and pulling in known hoods, to check their potential involvement. At this point, infamous 'ardman 'Mad' Frankie Fraser claims he paid a bribe to keep the cops away, although he was already a wanted man for other crimes. Can we call him 'Mad Frankie' nowadays? He did torture people, admittedly, but 'Neurologically Diverse Frankie' seems a more modern way to name him. He said he declined to get involved with the robbery as he had too much on his plate. His future girlfriend's mum had knitted the gang's balaclavas, complete with wonky eyeholes, but that was as close as Neurologically Diverse Frankie got to the action.

A detective I spoke to helpfully gave me the three simple ingredients for a perfect crime – do it once, take only cash and tell no one. The gang had done this before (more on that in a bit), they did only take cash but they did tell quite a few people. So they were only a third of the way to the perfect crime. Roy was caught with a colossal amount of cash in a bag, even though he knew the police were closing in. This isn't the action of someone who made one tiny slip, and should have gotten away with it. This is a proper clanger.

With his in mind, and getting more correspondence from people about his life, I begin to question Roy's motives for getting involved. Was it the thrill of the risk?! He couldn't continue to turn up in the best racing cars money could buy without someone asking what money he'd used to buy them.

Drug smuggler and top-flight American racer Randy Lanier was caught when winning some massive races with the best team and the best cars but with no legal way of funding it. You'll find an interesting documentary about him on Amazon somewhere. He's out now after decades in jail. I swapped friendly messages with him, without really knowing what I wanted to know. He's promoting medicinal marijuana now and keen to race again. He seems quite annoyed as he was 'only' smuggling what he calls 'a plant'. He made a mountain of money from crime. I asked if he knew Bernie, but didn't get an answer.

In film spoiler terms, we are now at the Titanic/iceberg interface moment; the Great Train Robbery. Not the St. Trinian's film version, the Nazi-funded book version, my YouTube thing filmed at the Great Central Railway with a blagged Jag or the movie version called Buster with Phil Collins – described by Radio Times as 'too squeaky clean to be believable'. On the assumption that you've heard the story before, I'll give you the following crash course in Roy's involvement:

He was a member of one of two gangs which had merged to form the team. I imagine the job description for his role would have been described thus: '*Wanted: Temporary general assistant to perform nightshifts in logistics in financial redeployment operation. Driving licence essential. Knowledge of railway signals, train carriage couplings and military and high-performance vehicles useful. Ability to keep schtum a distinct advantage. Apply in writing to Bruce Reynolds, London*'.

Roy was technically interested in a lot of the operation, even though he didn't necessarily need to be. He was the man who nobbled the lights to make the train stop at the bridge where the gang was waiting. He was the man who helped uncouple the Royal Mail carriages. He was on standby to drive the train into position should their own driver, Stan, not manage it. Stan fumbled his role and the frightened train driver got walloped. This attack on the driver was never in the plan and later helped to turn public opinion against the gang. No one was charged with his attack and both the gang and the police knew who it was, but there was insufficient evidence against him. There was a delay in the vacuum system which controlled the brakes and, when instructed to move the train again, the driver couldn't 'get pressure'. This might have been down to how Roy had connected the lines.

Roy then helped to shift the mail sacks down the embankment and load them into the truck below. Someone told the terrified train crew to 'stay there for at least half an hour', which led police to later rightly work out that the gang would be hiding nearby. The gang bailed out of the hideout prematurely, with Roy shuttling about with cash, sometimes in his Jaguar Mark 2, and, from there, they all dispersed and went into hiding on their own. Roy's 'whack' was roughly £163k of the £2.6 million. There had been a bit of a squabble over who was owed what, but Roy would not have complained at his share. A 'whack' was a percentage share, a 'drink' was a sizeable sum payable as a thank you.

At the time of the robbery, Roy was living in that nice flat on the top floor of Nell Gwynne House in Chelsea. A. G. Ogden described Nell Gwynn House as a 'pied a terre for many Chelsea bachelors who honor the spirit of Charles II'. I have the flat number and wrote to the address to ask who lives there now (they'll know that Roy once lived there), mentioning that lots of famous people live in the building and asking if they're a lion tamer or astronaut or something cool, and admitting that I didn't expect them to reply. I had really hoped for a 'Made in Chelsea' type to answer, endlessly stroking their hair while pouting and talking about their feelings. I got a nice old lady who didn't know much about it, using the place as a pied-à-terre on her stays in the city. Roy's neighbours included Bruce Forsythe (who was a bit of a diva, apparently), Diana Dors, a member of the SAS, actors and other interesting people. The gang met here a few times, and once held a vote on who would be members of the train robbery gang. Roy voted against Ronnie Biggs, but the vote carried and Biggs was in.

I was passing the place recently when I went to fetch milk and wandered off course by a few counties. I was excited to see Ted Bovis (actor Paul Shane) from the sitcom Hi-de-Hi! emerging from the front door, clutching a Sainsbury's carrier bag and struggling with a vape. When I shared this snippet with my girlfriend, she pointed out that he had died a decade earlier. I did see one of those chefs from the Two Fat Ladies show, who, my girlfriend explained, would have been either Jennifer Paterson or Clarissa Dickson Wright, who are also both dead. She then showed me a picture of Rosemary Shrager and asked if that was who I'd actually seen, which it was, but that's all an anticlimax to me after the ghost of Ted Bovis, who I long to see walk into a scene of Made in Chelsea, wearing his string vest and clutching his carrier bag talking about his feelings.

Chapter 30 – '63, Ungentlemanly

The first half of '63 was no less exciting than the second for Roy. But for the right reasons. Just two weeks before the robbery, he was racing his Brabham BT6 in Formula Libre, probably at Brands Hatch. He had been 2nd on the grid and won, his second win in Formula Libre that season. Perhaps a motorsport historian will unearth a sheaf of old results and correct me there, but that's what I think. I also think that he might have cheated, a bit. This class of car was supposed to have standardized engine sizes.

I spoke to a mechanic of the time and asked why Roy was so fast, and there was a hint that the engine might not have been the humble 1,100cc thing from Ford that was stipulated, but something saucier. There has been no shortage of cheating like this in motorsport history, and I have nothing to prove this 'don't quote me, but...' theory, but boring out the engine to a greater capacity was a not uncommon trick. So if they all did it, Roy included, then it's still a genuine win, right? I think it was Frankie Boyle who complained about drug testing in sport, saying we'd all actually love to see athletes illegally boosted to comic proportions, competing at ridiculous speeds. Fair or foul, Roy was very, very fast.

As our protagonist was enjoying racing, the train robbery gang were formulating the plan of the robbery. They met in The Star Tavern in Belgravia, 'a bolthole for the bourgeois', famous for having a gambling landlord called Paddy Kennedy who had a sharp tongue. He once told Elizabeth Taylor 'get your fat arse off that stool and let my friend sit down'. The Star Tavern is located near the German, Austrian and Serbian embassies (the Axis of Adolfs) in Belgravia. I visited. I learned that Lucky Terry Hogan was a regular and the landlord let the gang use the room upstairs for private meetings, although the gang never met in groups of more than four people for security reasons. Sometimes there are talks here on the Great Train Robbery. The chap who gives the talks is ex-CID and was generous with his time, but didn't teach me anything new about Roy. Today, The Star Tavern serves butternut squash and pine nut Wellington and has a sustainability policy. Please tell your server if you have any allergies. But it must have been so rock and roll in here, in Roy's day.

In June, Roy won his final ever Formula Junior race at Aintree in the BT6. By the end of the '63 season, Formula Junior was discontinued and racers went to the similar Formula Three or Formula Libre or Atlantic. That summer, Roy and others went to do a recce of the robbery site. Roy took his Jaguar Mark2 and the whole gang ate in a pub in the little village of Brill. As if this ugly mob of 'ard London gangsters arriving in Jaguars wasn't conspicuous enough, they left a huge tip. 'Meticulously planned'? Pah!

Roy drove at Brands in May and Snetterton in April, finishing on pole and setting the fastest lap in the Brabham. I met a gentleman called Jeremy Bouckley, one of the very few surviving racers from that era, who kindly added some colour to these results.

Jeremy is lovely chap and I'm grateful for his patience when I finally tracked him down in the West Midlands. Jeremy said that this was the golden era of racing. Formula Junior was just about affordable to the everyman, but was serious enough to be a solid step into the world of fast, single-seater racing. He was a printer, towing his car behind the works van. He recalls Roy arriving at races with a bunch of heavies in long, dark coats, looking a bit flash and (from Jeremy's tone) I think they were mildly threatening without actually threatening anyone. Roy was always very fast, but also careless, perhaps showing that he could afford the crashes that others couldn't. Jan Lammers had talked about the same 'elbows out' technique, the intention to come first at all costs, braking later and something about turning in and apexes that Brodie also said.

Jeremy said, in a very courteous, gentle manner, 'he was not very nice'. I pictured a scene of heavies and Jags and shooters, expecting some tale of people being disemboweled in the pits or something. But Jeremy said that Roy overtook him on the public road, Jeremy pulling his race car on a trailer behind his printers van and Roy thundering past pulling his own trailer with a Jaguar in an 'ungentlemanly' manner. On one hand, I was pleased because the thought of someone being properly unkind to lovely old Jeremy made me sad. On the other hand, it wasn't the juicy exposé I expected.

It was rare for Roy to mix gangster life with racing life in any case. I don't think the heavies turned up often. Jeremy also shared some spectacular man maths about how to afford racing back then, which almost had me reaching for my First Direct app and eBay. Something about 'pro rata' costs and value retention and things. Roy didn't have to worry about any of that.

Roy also raced in Ireland. There were plenty of races in the UK, so his regular trips to the Republic seem a little out of place to me, unless he had personal connections there or some other reason to race. Phoenix Park was a circuit in a public park in Dublin, a great city, but not a great circuit compared to others much closer to home. Perhaps there was some surreptitious Vic Lee-style smuggling going on, or maybe I'm overthinking it. Vic Lee was a team manager who was busted for drug smuggling, dragging a huge car transporter to Zandvoort near Amsterdam to take cars for testing when he could have quite easily done it much closer to home in the UK. A customs officer who was also a motorsport fan rumbled him. Twice-convicted Vic once said 'I'm proof that the prison system works.' Right-ho, Vic.

Roy did just love to drive. He used Booth Poole garage in Islandbridge as a base for the Dublin race weekend. It was a Wolseley Cars dealership, used by other racers, where they could set up and tune the cars ready for the race nearby. Roy drove his single seater to the circuit on public roads and was stopped by the police. I can relate to this. I was stopped when taking my three children to school in a two-seater Caterham once (or twice). 'Rich,' said the copper, 'I can't keep turning a blind eye to this sort of thing', before turning a blind eye again. Roy was light-heartedly admonished for having no tax or insurance. I think a few drivers did the same that weekend.

He did well in the race, beating hotshot Jackie Stewart, and everyone else, to collect a trophy from Sir Basil Goulding. Sir Baz was an art collector, keen champion of Irish causes, cricketer and RAF officer who, I was disappointed to find, did not have a massive moustache. His son, Lingard, went on to lead a similarly interesting life but with added motorsport on top, once hitting almost 200 mph at Monza in a Formula 5000 car. Roy's tally of 16 wins plus 11 fastest laps put him in the frame for some sponsorship money from Esso, which would start in '64. At the same time, his oldest friend, Micky Ball, was sent to jail for 5 years and Roy was sitting on quite a bit of cash.

This is the point in my research, and in this book, at which we realise that Roy was not the Robin Hood character I'd hoped for, nor a misguided young man dragged down the wrong path in life by others. He had everything at his fingertips at this point in '63; sufficient money to live, a great career in racing, honest sponsorship money for the future and a fantastic flat in Nell Gwynne House. OK, Ted Bovis probably didn't live next door, but things were good.

There is no evidence to suggest that he was coerced into doing the train robbery and, as we now know, even after that, there was no sign he'd ever go straight for long. He was a rogue. So now the working title of my book morphs from 'The Real Weasel, train robber and racer' to 'The Real Weasel, train robber, racer, rogue'.

Chapter 31 – '62, SEXI

The '60s was a great time to be alive. Jeremy Bouckley talked of the summer of love, of great music, new colours, hot girls and happy people. The Beatles, Twiggy, the Stones, Concorde and Bluebird made the news. There was the first man in space, the first heart transplant and the first man on the Moon. On the roads, Jaguar launched the E-Type, the Mini became an instant style icon and the Rover 2000 was the first European car of the year – but my Dad bought a Ford Anglia all the same. Mods and rockers added excitement at the beach. England won some football thing. Life was good.

In Formula One, the regulations shifted from a maximum engine size of 1.5 litres to 3 litres and the interest in motorsport rapidly grew around the world. That young woman, Michelle, who had written to Roy in jail, was driving a Mini at Crystal Palace with a registration plate that read 'SEXI'. It's so easy to be sucked into the excitement of this era, the Swinging Sixties.

In December '62, Roy saw Denny Hulme racing in a Brabham and decided he was going to have one. He went to Motor Racing Developments Ltd., in Byfleet, who made them. An overenthusiastic and undereducated YouTuber (me) once said that Roy emptied a briefcase full of cash on Ron Tauranac's desk and bought a Brabham BT6 on the spot. Only, that didn't quite happen, but it'll perhaps appear in print in someone else's book at some point. I know this because, at the time, the tea boy and general workshop dogsbody was a young man called Nick Goozee, who is now retired and living in Dorset, and he recently told me about those early days at Brabham.

If I can cram Nick's fascinating life into one, overly long sentence, it would say he was the son of an RAF officer who started hanging around the Brabham garage as a kid in the hope of meeting his hero, Jack Brabham, did some summer work and later an apprenticeship there, his career later progressed to Penske where he eventually became managing director and oversaw teams in NASCAR, Formula One, CART and other sports car series worldwide. He, like Jeremy and others from that era I spoke to, was modest, very generous with his time and laughed to learn I'd been trolling Bernie by post.

But Roy didn't dump a suitcase of cash on Ron Tauranac's desk. We ought to cover bit of Brabham's history now: Jack Brabham was an Australian who came to the UK to develop his motorsport career, teaming up with fellow Aussie Ron Tauranac to build racing cars. Jack Brabham is the only man to ever win a Formula One World Championship in one of his own cars. In the '60s, Brabham was the world's leading manufacturer of racing cars and Nick would cycle there in the hope of meeting his hero, Jack Brabham.

Nick said that there was a hard-working, open atmosphere at Brabham, with customers coming in and out and mechanics and engineers mingling directly with customers and drivers. The boss, Ron, rarely dealt directly with the customers. He was, by nature, quite a shy sort of chap and had a salesman deal with the money side of things. In the autumn of '63, Nick was an apprentice and working all hours. He said this was, to him, nirvana; working on cars and mixing with drivers he'd worshipped as a boy.

I could not pass up this opportunity to ask about Bernie who bought the Brabham company in '72. Nick said he was working late, as was common in the industry, when the phone rang in the workshop at approximately 10 pm. A voice asked 'who's that?', to which Nick replied 'It's me, Nick, but who are you asking me that?' Bernie said he'd just bought the company, before hanging up. The next morning, it was business as usual, until Ron sheepishly pulled the staff together and introduced Bernie and his sidekick Colin Seeley as the new owners.

Nick diplomatically explained to me that Ron had perhaps had his trousers pulled down, and Ron was gently squeezed out of the company by Bernie, who wanted things done his own way. Bernie installed a timer on the light switch in the toilets and did deals from cars parked outside the factory with what sounded like some rather spicy types of people.

Brabham employed a chap called Len Wimhurst, who was ex-SAS and lived in the rough New Cross part of London. Len mixed with Roy and 'his type', said Nick. Nick and Len were probably chalk and cheese socially, but close in the workplace. Len would sometimes give Nick a lift, and Nick recalled an instance of some low-level road rage on the way to work and Len calmly getting out of their car and, with minimal effort, chopping the other motorist to the ground in one smooth movement, before carrying on the journey as normal. Nick said Len was immensely strong and would often have contraband from friends who worked down the docks. He had great talent in the workshop and once built a single-seat racing car in the street outside his own house, before designing his own car, called Palliser, which showed great potential.

After Bernie, Brabham ended up in the hands of another tax fiddler, Joachim Lüthi, before running out of money and collapsing in '92. But Brabham of the '60s was a cracking company and at the heart of a burgeoning motorsport world. And into this scene comes Roy, who dealt with an intermediary, not Ron, and later took delivery of a very, very competitive racing car. No one asked where the money came from. Which is good, because it came from a robbery.

Chapter 32 – '62, OOO

Gordon Goody was a baddie. So was Roy, and so was Charlie White. They were great train robbers together. 'Lucky Terry' Hogan was also a great train robber (using an alias and never caught). Micky Ball, of Lambrook Terrace, Fulham, probably would have been a train robber too, but he was in jail, the only one convicted for a robbery all of them participated in, in November '62. Ball was nicked just three weeks after the robbery and, considering this team also did the 'well-planned' train robbery, they left a trail of pretty obvious clues behind. The judge called the robbery an 'entirely successful enterprise', although Ball would not have agreed with his assessment, as he got 5 years inside for it. The others got away, and a chunk of the stolen money ended up in the till at Brabham as Roy drove off in his BT6.

Let's rewind to November '62 and Eaton Square, Belgravia, which was posh then and is posh today. I know this because I visited, this time with my back covered by my trusty aide to workplace shirking, called 'out of office' (OOO). OOO might imply holiday or essential business travel or sick leave or something. OOO doesn't need any more explanation than those three words. I would abbreviate it to those three letters if I could – anything to avoid overexertion at work. I was OOO because I wanted to see how easy it is, even today, to steal a car from here and, to cut to the chase, it would be very easy indeed.

148

Britain's most stolen car, depending on which bit of the internet you read, is the Range Rover. Here, in Eaton Square, there are dozens of the things. Parked wheels on kerb and yet still sticking into the road, on double yellows and on pedestrian crossings, sometimes with hazard lights on, which, dear owner, does not make your illegal parking invisible. Autocar reports that three of the top ten stolen car models in Britain today are Range Rovers and Land Rovers. All you need is some whizz-kid with a laptop and an aerial of some kind and you're away, it seems. I don't know what it is with the Marmite appeal of Range Rovers. Personally, I think there was something amusing in the words of its inventor, Spen King, who said at the time of its launch, 'I think people are going to learn to look on their cars as less of a prestige symbol and more as an absolute necessity to living', predicting the exact opposite of what I see in Belgravia.

A short mews street has cars that are much more my cup of tea. An Alfa Romeo Spider, a classic Mercedes SL, a BMW Isetta and a couple of classic Jaguars. These are outside Belgravia Garage, which is one of the oldest garages in the UK, serving the well-heeled since there was horse muck and carts everywhere. There's a lift to an underground garage and hot cars with keys in. Now, I am not suggesting visiting and driving off in one of their customer's lovely machines, you'd be caught on camera pretty quickly, but I did wonder if the owner would just make an insurance claim and go back to their day of eating caviar off a supermodel's bum and counting their millions if I did nick one,

The BMW Isetta I saw looks to be the perfect car for the city – it's less than half the length of a Range Rover, in fact it's almost as long as the Range Rover is wide. The Isetta has seating for 100% more people than I saw in each Range Rover as I skulked around Belgravia. It is constructed from such flimsy material that driving one would make you as vulnerable (and, therefore, as considerate) as any cyclist. And, forgetting emissions and boring technicalities, it's just much, much nicer to look at in places like this.

Roy rightly knew there'd be easy picking here and snaffled the 3.8-litre Jaguar Mark 2 of American actor Craig Stevens, who, Google tells me, was relaxing in London after filming a series called 'Man of the World – gets his Jag nicked'. Well, it was half-called that. Overcome by inverse snobbery and right-on opinions best left to the vacuum of social media, I skulked back to work, logged back on and thanked my silent sidekick, OOO.

Chapter 33 – '62, Suits you

Roy removed one of the rear seats of Craig Stevens' Jag and welded in a large steel box with a cover. He had learned the movements of the wages delivery from a nearby Barclays bank to the BOAC airline at Heathrow Airport. The gang got fitted for suits. Roy was always a smart dresser, but the trip to the tailor sounded like a sketch from The Fast Show's 'suits you' routine, and the gang had a fit of the giggles and the tailor remembered them as a rum bunch. I appreciate there's a bit of 'a friend said' and 'someone told me', but getting people to put their name to this was a bit of a minefield and, honestly, wouldn't add much more than we already know other than some people get overly litigious and I can't afford a lawyer.

Wearing these city gentlemen suits, they went to a DIY shop in Uxbridge and asked for the biggest bolt croppers they had. They were also spotted wandering outside the airport perimeter in their fancy suits by a passing lorry driver. They went to a newsagent and bought a copy of the Daily Mail, which, even though I haven't seen it, was bound to have had a feature about how eating food will give you cancer and, inevitably, something unpleasant about foreigners. The shop owner remembers wondering what such suits would want with his ironmongery and noted their car registration number.

They then loitered near the business lounge, were noticed reading the noticeboard and then pounced when the wages van unloaded outside the lift doors. The van crew were heavily coshed. The money was loaded into the Jag, which then sprinted over the airfield and burst through the 'crash gate', which had had its padlock snipped the previous night. From there onto Bath Road and into the dark streets of London. They had netted £62,500, which was equivalent to 78 years' worth of the average worker's wage. Quite a haul. They were in and out in a flash.

My position on a potential life of crime at this point shifts a little. I've sort of forgotten the later violence in Roy's life and imagined the thrill of this robbery. Rerunning this crime in my mind, I am spurred at the joy of ignoring the £12.50 a day ULEZ charge to get to Heathrow, no £16 parking charge for the little time it took Roy to load the loot, no ANPR and no traffic. Comet House was the building where the crime took place, which is now no longer there, but it would have required entry to the building, which, today, means buying an airline ticket and all the online fannying that ensues. No bags, no priority boarding, no fees for picking a damned seat. No boarding pass on your phone that won't scan because it's a phone not a boarding pass, no queues for some cold-faced child to charge you £20 to print. No queues in security or liquids in a bag. No miles and miles of shuffling queues. And the greatest offence to all passengers at Heathrow, or any airport – the duty-free shop.

The duty-free shop is a psychopath-designed maze; wall-to-wall crap designed to guilt-trip the traveller into buying their children chocolate, shiny floors forcing you to walk slowly, hairpin corners at the perfume section to throw you, stumbling into the shelves of ridiculous stink, seating areas with insufficient seating designed to coerce you to sit (and pay) in the 'restaurants' onsite.

On one hand, I must admire the huge lengths they have gone to extract money from the tired traveller at every turn. On the other hand, I have a screaming urge to smash a stolen Jaguar through the whole rotten hellhole of it all and hoof it down the motorway with a bootful of cash, trailing miles of Tensabarrier behind me.

Days after the robbery, police said six of the eight men were known to them, then the Jag was recovered with the Daily Mail in it and, a few days later, they set up an identity parade at Canon Row Police Station, where only Micky Ball was picked out. Ball was described as a 'credit agent' and paid a £5,000 bail, reporting to police daily, before being sent to jail in March of the following year, when the gang were planning the train robbery and Roy was treating himself to new cars. Ball said in court, 'I was there and I'll take my punishment.' Roy got off, as did Gordon Goodie, Charlie Wilson and Lucky Charlie, who went straight after this and raised a family, but never found true happiness.

Chapter 34 – '62, Cooper

Also late in '62, someone got away with robbing a train. A different train. The newspapers reported it as 'The Great Train Robbery', which was the name of a 1903 film and wasn't the train robbery we all know about. Someone pulled the emergency cord of the London to Cheltenham train and hopped off with £760 in cash in a Royal Mail sack. No one was caught for this crime. This story fits with a similar stunt Roy would pull much later in life, but I suspect he was not personally involved because it chronologically overlaps with the wages job at Heathrow.

Earlier in '62, there was an aborted robbery which Roy *was* involved in. The idea of robbing trains was being discussed amongst London's criminals; it's mentioned in a book about Charlie Wilson, for example. They had a postal worker who was working late shifts at a rail marshalling yard identify the carriages used to transport the high-value packages (known as HVPs). From there, they got a good description of the kind of sack used. And then they looked at timings and locations, deciding that Weybridge in Surrey would be a good spot to stop a train, steal the HVPs and scarper into the night in cars.

This is a very similar modus operandi to the Great Train Robbery and would have served as a handy practice run. Two Jaguar cars were stolen to order, almost certainly by Roy, and prepped for high performance.

Now, the daft video I made years ago states that Roy robbed Jaguar's Le Mans performance department at the factory in Coventry, to get the best bits for his own road car. I 'learned' this from a comment on an internet forum where maniacs and fantasists waste lots of pixels arguing over literally nothing. But some of the comments were particularly detailed and revealed a great in-depth knowledge of how Jaguar's 3.4 engines were stronger than the 3.8 engines, and how the 3.4 model handled better. This I believe to be true. Roy also paid people to pinch bits for him. This is also true. But I don't think he went to the huge length of going to Coventry to steal bits which would give only small performance gains for a road car that just needed to be quicker than the police. Roy already knew he was faster than any driver the police had ever sent after him. Jag weren't using the same kind of car in their Le Mans team anyway.

The internet might give some morsels we can use here, but it also spews a bellyful of honk over everything most of the time. And I'm sorry that some of that honk may have come from my own nauseous innards again. So, Roy gets these two Jaguars and stores them in a lock-up near Weybridge and, just before the heist, someone steals them both before the gang arrive. Friends of Roy's from later life, like Brodie, would passionately deny Roy would ever rob his own gang. I am not so sure. He had friends in the motor trade who could easily shift the two stolen cars and pay him, after he'd been paid to source (steal) them in the first place. It looks like Roy was paid twice for the same cars. Passengers chuffing though Weybridge would have no idea of the drama they escaped.

Many of the facts about Roy's life can be precisely dated. The train robbery, for example, court appearances, having an après-ski drink with Brodie and crashing Renault hatchbacks in front of a crowd. Some are a bit vaguer and others simply random anecdotal bits I've lobbed into the text with gay abandon. One fairly important chunk of the story is simply dated '1960s', so I'll just shoehorn it in here now.

You're probably familiar with the Mini Cooper and, if you're a car saddo like me, will know that the name originates from John Cooper, a man who tuned fast Minis and built racing cars back then. I emailed his son to ask to verify something I'd read and, considering it's quite a tender subject, I was not entirely surprised at the lack of reply. And I understand why. John had given Roy some driving lessons in his single seaters in either the late '50s or early '60s, and John's son was a young lad at the time. He remembers little of the incident, but it appears that someone had burgled their works office and stolen some of their trophies. Then someone tried to extort the Cooper family. The children's lives were threatened. The family managed to get word to the police via a relative. John Cooper put the ransom money into a bag and drove to the rendezvous point as instructed. Crouching in the back of the car (a Mini Cooper!) were two strapping coppers who, when they arrived at the designated drop-off point for the money, leapt from the car and bundled the crook to the ground. I am not sure that anyone was actually punished for this in the end.

Brodie vehemently denied Roy having had anything to do with this. It's worth pointing out that Brodie hadn't even met Roy by this time, and the Coopers suspected him. Although he was more of a robber than a burglar in later years, his earlier crimes were more of the breaking and entering type that follows the crime at the Coopers' place. Around the same time, he ordered one of the very first Jaguar E-Types, allegedly chassis number 32, which was one of just 56 demonstrator cars Jaguar delivered to their UK dealer network.

He was still living in Doneraile Street, Fulham, and had gotten the bug for karting, which is the first step many take before jumping into more hardcore motorsport. In '62, he represented Great Britain at karting at an event in France, winning four out of five races, having gotten the karting bug a couple of years earlier at Tilbury in Essex, under the tutelage of a man called Big Dean who, with such a name, was only ever going to work at a karting place in Essex. He was already committing crime to fund this.

Chapter 35 – '50s, Milk float

Brodie had confirmed that Roy had repeatedly been in the south of France over the years, and there is one public photograph of Roy with Micky Ball, what might be Lucky Terry Hogan and others from their wider group, which, considering Ball cut his ties with Roy soon after the airport robbery, dates it to the very early '60s. It's a group of men and women, looking very smart, dressed for dinner and sat around a long table 'in France'. There are shirts and ties, jewellery and smart hairstyles, with everyone smiling. At the same time there were a number of hotel and casino robberies, which took the local authorities by surprise. The casinos were run by mobsters who tended not to rob each other, preferring to rinse the gamblers instead, and so when they were robbed, no one could work out who had done it and the local mobsters all turned on each other.

Roy supposedly did some cat burgling, stealing jewels from wealthy old ladies, aristocrats and actors and actresses who were 'resting' in between assignments. There is no way, on their normal trajectory in life, that any of Roy's group of friends would have been able to afford such a holiday and the fact they all looked so comfortable in such surroundings indicated it wasn't their first trip either. This looks like hiding in plain sight. One robbery alone netted a reported £144,000. From there, Roy would drive up to Switzerland in his Mercedes and exchange the francs and other foreign currency he'd taken into money orders and sterling, ready for use back home.

Brodie tells a story about Roy hiding a diamond inside the headlamp lens of the Merc and a customer's officer staring at it for some time, trying to work out if it was some new lighting technology or something. I can't believe he'd hide a diamond so big that someone standing a few feet away would notice it inside a headlamp, but Brodie is a great storyteller and he would be telling this second hand, repeating what his mate Roy would have told him a quarter of a century later. I feel that Roy liked telling a story, when safe amongst friends. He seldom told these to fellow racers or people in the motoring world, preferring to keep those lives separate. Roy and his friends went karting in the south of France, where they'd go to hide after committing crimes in London, until the karting venue owner got fed up with them smashing the karts up all the time. So Roy bought the kart venue on the understanding that it would be his playground and that he'd sell it back to the owner when he went back to England. This arrangement worked quite well.

Roy told a story that his gang would buy expensive biscuits just for the tins. They would then feed the biscuits to the seagulls and store their stolen goods in the empty tins, which would be buried in the hills above Nice. Some were never retrieved. In learning this, and remembering the story of the machine gun in the garden in Surrey, I feel that Roy left a trail of biscuit crumbs for others to follow on a kind of treasure hunt. It feels like he told these stories to Brodie and others out of mischief. Or, perhaps, there's genuinely 'gold in them there hills'.

In the late '50s, Roy had already served time in jail and, at the time of the Great Train Robbery, had six convictions for theft, receiving stolen goods, shop-breaking and various motoring offences. Once, on his release, he briefly had a job as a milkman and would let the local kids steal milk from the back of the milk float for fun. He would steal cars with his mate Micky Ball. Everyone who was associated with this is now dead and the crimes weren't big enough to be reported in the major newspapers of the time, so I had a rummage on the British Newspaper Archive again. This is a fantastic resource, but is very sensitive to data input.

A morning of sniffing through ancient regional newspapers and local press cuttings found what I thought was info on these crimes, but no; 'a man in Mickey Mouse pyjamas was arrested with three others from a Mercedes A Class minutes after an alleged car theft in Tamworth' was funnier than it was relevant to my search. A very well-respected journo from the world of Formula One World Championship, called Joe Saward, once wrote that Roy was a 'top waterskier'. This was another fact that I simply couldn't square with what I thought I knew of Roy when I first starting writing this book, but one that became more plausible the more I learned of his life. It's not unreasonable to assume that waterskiing is a rich man's sport; you need a boat, a lake, all the kit, it just didn't seem likely that a young Roy from Fulham would have access to such a sport.

I then remember that Brodie told me he'd done downhill skiing with Roy and a (short-lived) girlfriend he had in the '80s. I found a photograph which showed Roy not only waterskiing, but going over a jump one-handed, smiling. I focused on the 'top' bit of 'top waterskier' and had also heard him described as a 'champion', and emailed the very helpful British Waterski Association (BWA), who offered to check their records. Competitive waterskiing is a fairly new thing, it seems, and there are no records of English competitions that Roy might have been involved in, in south-east England in the late '50s. Still, he could definitely ski, even though the BWA drew a blank. I can understand the appeal of motorsport, that's where I first found Roy, but *waterskiing*?

Chapter 36 – '50s, Arthur Longbottom

'Canal Street', says the sign that leads to the canal on the outskirts of Leicester, not to some back-door reward for suburban gay men, as the vandals would sometimes have you believe. At the end of this street is a series of lakes formed from old gravel pits where the local waterski club meets. One lake is named after John Merrick, who I had always assumed was the local 'sleb better known as the Elephant Man, which confused me as I doubted the poor bugger was known for his water sports skills. No, that's Joseph Merrick (no relation) and the lake is named after a local who was an Olympic sailor. It's not too far from my home.

It's February as I type this and I thought I should at least try to see what waterskiing is like, to try and understand the appeal to Roy, to understand what made him tick. Just to recap, I'm in Leicester, in February, and it's a gravel pit. The local club were very friendly but explained that they don't really start until April. I could pay a tenner to join as a casual member, then it's '£15 per tow'. I am sure there are health and safety matters and equipment to be hired, but was disappointed that it is so cheap to waterski here as it removes an excuse I had for not trying it. While waiting for April to come around, and the surroundings to be a bit more Mediterranean, I looked for more reasons not to waterski.

This lake is fed by the River Soar, which flows along just lovely, says Wikipedia, until 'there is a significant decrease in the quality… where the Wanlip sewage treatment works enters the river'. That's a very short distance from here.

Putting water quality aside (Liv Garfield, Severn Trent's CEO, earns over £3 million a year and was described by the parliamentary Environmental Audit Committee as 'disingenuous'; you won't see her waterskiing often), there's the danger of the boats.

Californian research from '77 says that there were 9.6 deaths per 100,000 'crafts' when waterskiing. I assume crafts means 'attempts'. This data includes one instance of 'near-fatal amputation' and some photographs of someone who appears to have had their arse chopped off by a propeller. So, that's a one in ten thousand chance I will come to some harm down this street – more if you include predatory homosexuals drawn here by the signage. I need no further excuse to avoid reliving this little part of Roy's life. We'll just trust that waterskiing can be fun and look into his other hobbies, like football.

Joe Saward had mentioned that Roy had had a trial for QPR football club. I had read a prison letter that Roy wrote in the early '70s encouraging a friend to support Chelsea and admiring the skills of Charlie Cooke, who had signed for a club record of £72,000 in '66. Cooke ended his career playing for the Dallas Sidekicks, having also played for the Calgary Boomers. Where do they get these stupid names from? It makes Cockney gangster names seem positively sensible. It was time to look into football.

I started a correspondence with QPR's historian. There are, he helpfully told me, 'two players still alive from that era who should remember Roy playing'. This got me excited. I was ready, finger hovering over OOO, ready to escape to a football ground to talk to some nonagenarians about Roy and 'goalposts for jumpers'. I was even googling the team fixtures, players and general history. I know bugger all about football and was suddenly excited to learn. 'But...' on went the historian, 'both of them have Alzheimer's disease and don't even know they were ever footballers, let alone remember other players.' I was as deflated as a Sports Direct football on the roof of a flat-roofed pub. 'We recently lost Arthur Longbottom', he said, assuming I knew who Longbottom was. I'd watch more football if they all had such great names. Perhaps I had the wrong club.

Doneraile Street is very close to Fulham's ground. I emailed them to ask and didn't officially get far but, and this is a big but, someone said he'd had a trial for Fulham's under 18s and got released after repeatedly breaking a rule that said no player was allowed to arrive by motorbike as they were considered too dangerous. This sounds *exactly* like our Roy. But having done some homework, and had a few hints that there was a connection with the football club and a criminal matching Roy's description, I eventually ended up learning about a neighbour of Roy's from Fulham called 'Taters'.

'Taters in the mould' is cockney rhyming slang for cold, and George Henry 'Taters' Chatham earned his nickname for his cool, unflappable approach. He was more than 20 years older than Roy and was known in Fulham for his skill as a burglar. Taters did have a trial for QPR but wasn't good enough. I was annoyed as this meant my QPR research about Roy's potential football career had been for nothing. Facts like Queens Park Rangers (of London) are not the same as Queens Park (of Scotland), for example, and asking questions of such stupidity quickly use up the goodwill of put-upon club historians. I even bought a bloody QPR car sticker off eBay. Their nickname is 'The Hoops' and they were the first team in England to install an AstroTurf pitch, and then the first to remove one. Hashtag fun fact.

I've had to learn all this, so I'm sharing it with you whether you like it or not. At the time of writing, they sit between Huddersfield Athletic United and Sheffield Villa PLC in the football league, or something. But streaking across the plastic pitch of my research, now, comes Bernie Ecclestone.

I apologise for putting the image of that naked little goblin in your head – it's a metaphor. Bernie and fellow Formula One World Championship 'character' Flavio Briatore bought QPR in 2007 in a rare for Bernie 'investment' move. That's two pairs of legally compliant inverted commas in one sentence, you will notice. In 2010, Bernie said 'It's mainly commercial things and for me to see if we can get that working better', which seemed sensible enough, before concluding 'once you get me involved that's it. I'm there' and then bailing out. To cheer myself up, I anonymously posted the QPR sticker to Bernie's office and then panicked remembering that Bernie was caught illegally carrying a gun recently.

Bernie's and Roy's world overlap so many times, it's easy to see why Roy tapped him up in later life, but Roy didn't play for QPR, Taters did. Taters is the link with the football club and his life entwines with Roy's in other ways. He was a close associate of a friend of Roy's, Lucky Hogan, and must have inspired the young Roy with some of the outrageous crimes he committed. This is a man who shaped Roy's criminal habits.

Chapter 37 – '50s, Taters

Taters came from a middle-class family and would read society magazines to research potential victims. Roy, you may remember, did the same in later life. Taters once stole two jewelled swords belonging to the Duke of Wellington, and something called a chelengk, which looks like a typo but is a kind of military award that had been given to Lord Nelson. He became addicted to gambling and his crime funded this. He once prised a large precious stone out of a military sword halfway through a game of cards and used it as his stake.

Taters was a prolific thief. He was hospitalised for six weeks in a fall while burgling the Countess of Dartmouth's house, returning to attempt to finish the job while still in plaster. He often teamed up with Peter 'Human Fly' Scott, a man of such confidence that, if disturbed during a burglary, he would call out, reassuringly, 'don't worry, it's only me!' Taters led an incredibly colourful life. He said 'I was a rebel against authority and I had no respect for the police. If I could outwit them in any way, I would.'

It's easy to see a young Roy being impressed by such men. Taters had owned a Lagonda and a Mercedes-Benz in his time, but, like Roy and other criminals, struggled to manage his money. Plus, he was a big gambler. He lived for years in abject poverty in a flat in Fulham. Of his victims, he said 'They were usually very, very rich people, millionaires. Some of them regarded it as a nice thing to talk about at dinner parties.' They say Taters stole goods to the value of £100 million in his time, attempting his final crime aged 81, just before his death. To a young man like Roy, from a poor family, having lived through the turmoil of war, well, you can see how these criminals became his peers.

One of Roy's first major crimes was a robbery he committed in a stolen Jaguar with his mate Micky Ball. And not just anyone's Jaguar, it belonged to Britain's first Formula One Championship winner, Mike Hawthorn. Mike had just won the title and Roy had envied his Jag for some time and, when the opportunity arose, he stole it. He kept it in a garage in the East End of London, used false registration plates and seldom drove it. It was stolen for a specific robbery and Roy was never caught or charged. He returned the car after the robbery, parking it around the corner from a club that Hawthorn frequented, but reportedly stole the prestigious BRDC badge off the grill and kept it as a memento. In later years, this badge was returned and, I'm told, lives in the BRDC clubhouse in a display case today. I'm not allowed into the BRDC. I've waved my plywood 'Judges Choice' at the bloke on security and mimed my winning credentials at the window, but that door remains firmly closed to me.

Funnily enough, Nick Goozee is a member and told me that he barely recognises anyone there because he saw motorsport as a job and, I think, he's a modest sort of person who doesn't feel the need to chase famous people or look for trinkets stolen by our anti-hero decades ago. There is a twist to this crime of Roy's.

Very soon after Roy returned the car to Hawthorn, Hawthorn was involved in a bit of a race on public roads and subsequently died in a huge crash on the A3. He was ill and his condition led to occasional blackouts, plus the weather was bad, and there's no doubt that hooning about in a powerful Jaguar would have been great fun, but I have to wonder if it's the same Jag that Roy had nicked, and if he'd returned it in good shape with no mechanical maladies.

In the '50s, it is said that Roy served a long apprenticeship at Harrods of London, as a silversmith. Initial dialogue with Harrods' press department about his employment soon met dead ends when they realised who Roy was in later life. Roy has been dead for over a quarter of a century and so I do not have any first-hand correspondence with him; I was on the sofa at home when he died, barely knowing who he was. Much of what I've written comes from people he met, people I subsequently tracked down. Some were happy to share their names and personal details. Those people are mostly from the motorsport world who viewed him as a curiosity. Those who were able to talk to me about his criminal life did so mostly on the basis that I did not use their names or I had the feeling that me sharing their details might put me in a sticky spot, so kept things confidential. I can hide behind this nomdeplume, but it would be easy to find me, I suppose.

Roy was a private person, particularly in later life, but there are a few people he shared his personal stories with who retold them to me. Brodie's tomes are worth wading through for snippets of this, but they also provide cold facts that some of Roy's stories were dodgier than that Harrods statue of Dodi and Diana.

The second Burlington Arcade smash and grab, for example, it's a great story but impossible that Roy was there. Court dates, newspaper reports and other facts prove this. Roy talked quickly. He was an animated person in private company. Some stories are ones that he made up and told others, who repeated them. Others are stories that his friends misguidedly made up in later life. I feel that his Harrods employment is an example of this. There are no reports in the contemporary media of him ever having worked there. Tabloids are always looking for an angle and 'ex-Harrods employee robs train' would have sold lots of red tops at the time. Roy's supposed time at Harrods was only a decade before the Great Train Robbery. People would have remembered him, old colleagues, for example. But there's nothing on this. Roy was, however, undeniably a capable and enthusiastic silversmith, and this is not some self-taught skill. He knocked up silverware in prison toilets, so keen was he.

There are some good examples of Roy's work around. They bear his 'maker's mark', RJJ, Roy John James. His mark appears in the huge list of silversmiths between Robert John Harvey of Regent Street, registered in 1848, and Richard James Olivier, a watch case and pocket barometer maker of 1867, whose work now fetches quite hefty sums at auction. Silver made in London should also carry a lion passant symbol, other English towns and cities have their own symbols, although Roy didn't bother with this (unsurprisingly). The whole system today is a bit nonsense as silverware made in India can legally carry an anchor, meaning 'made in Birmingham', and silver from Italy can carry Sheffield's crown. Harrods' silver has 'H Ld' stamped on it, but this is very rare and confirms my thoughts that Harrods seldom made their own silverware and, therefore, Roy couldn't have been directly employed there, could he? There's no denying his considerable skill, regardless of where he learned it, or how.

Young lads from the rough end of London don't get ushered through the door at Harrods. They would have been suspicious of having someone like that under their prestigious roof. He once said 'you never, ever steal from your employer', but that's hardly something he'd put on a job application form anyway. Roy gravitated to Hatton Garden and I think he actually served his time there, not at Harrods. I'd quite like to repeat the Harrods story to burst their pompous bubble, or get it repeated somewhere else if someone uses this book as a reference in a 'Great Train Robbers – Their Secret Department Store Orgy in Aisle Three' version of events.

I am more of an Aldi shopper than Harrods, anyway. Aldi has never had a statue of Diana and Dodi Fayed holding hands while releasing an albatross but, at my local Aldi, there is occasionally a pigeon stuck in the doors. At the time of Roy's supposed employment there, someone had the wonderful job of sitting around waiting to be fired. If anyone complained about Harrods, their HR department would 'fire' that someone just to placate the customer. This person didn't do anything, just sat in a chair and drank tea, and after being 'fired' they'd walk out the door and straight back in, to be rehired in the same role.

I asked Brodie, one of very few people who appear in the part of the Venn diagram of Roy's life that is the overlap between racing and his tales of crime, why he would have left Harrods in Knightsbridge (or somewhere like Eric Ross' in Hatton Garden) to pursue crime. 'He was bored', he says. It's hard to argue with that. It's rather like the moment in '63 when he was on the cusp of a proper motorsport deal, with a winning streak behind him and money in the bank, and he stupidly committed the Great Train Robbery. It can only be the thrill of crime that turned Roy John James into Roy 'The Weasel' James.

In '55, Roy was 20. In later life, he told people that he'd served in Malaya when doing national service, that he was a crack shot with a .303 rifle and that he and a Scottish comrade helped save a local from death by running through the jungle carrying the sick man. I gently shook the Ancestry.com website, snapped branches off the National Service records database and chainsawed through forests of family trees to try and substantiate this, but there is no record of him having ever served. His motorsport gongs have survived, his helmet and other personal paperwork, so where are the service records? Getting shot at by insurgents and shouted at by sergeants doesn't seem like my idea of fun, nor Roy's either. He would have been eligible for National Service. Maybe he was in Ireland.

Chapter 38 – '52, Sir Baz

In '52, George Henry 'Taters' Chatham participated in the Eastcastle Street robbery with Lucky Hogan and it's not a huge leap of the imagination to see a 17-year-old Roy involved. Roy looked up to these men, moved in their circles and started getting rich around this time. He had already been involved in criminal activity with Micky Ball.

There was a gang of seven men who used two green saloon cars to sandwich a Post Office van and cosh the driver on this street near Soho and Chinatown. Near the Blue Posts pub, at 4 am, the gang launched their ambush. The same pub, I learned recently, has a 'no children and no phones or laptops' rule that sounds absolutely bloody brilliant to me. They stole a quantity of uncut diamonds destined for Hatton Garden and £287,000 in used notes (which today would scarcely stretch to a round of drinks and a bag of pork scratchings in the Blue Posts). The van had an alarm system which had been disabled. One car was later found near Regent's Park, with some of the mailbags being recovered untouched. The other car was cheekily parked near a police station.

The robbers knew exactly what they were looking for. Prime minister Winston Churchill demanded daily updates from the Postmaster General, Herbrand Edward Dundonald Brassey Sackville, 9th Earl De La Warr, GBE, PC, JP, DL, a man who probably didn't use his full name when answering the telephone. The police deployed over 1,000 officers but no one was ever caught. Comparing this crime to the Great Train Robbery, and looking at Roy's role in particular, I can see him in the driver's seat and smiling.

In the late '40s, Roy might have burgled the home of Sir Basil Henriques, known as Bernhard Baron House in East London. There's a blog online by someone called Dan Jones (a self-proclaimed artist and human rights campaigner) mentioning this. Today, it's fancy flats, but back then it was both the home of Henriques and a place where he and his wife charitably supported young lads from the area who needed some direction in life, by providing a social club. I don't want to believe Roy did this – he would have needed some direction in life at this point – but it was easy pickings. I have to remind myself that Roy did some pretty ugly things later in life, because I am now at the point where I'm sort of rooting for him and don't want to believe he was a rogue from such an early age.

Sir Baz was a British philanthropist of Portuguese Jewish origins with some views that were outdated at the time and positively archaic now. He said 'Women seem to think themselves rivals and equals to men in all things, but they are only superior in some things such as washing the baby and washing up.' He did a huge amount of good for deprived Jewish children, setting up a holiday home and social clubs. This was very close to the area that Roy was living with his mother. It was very deprived. Roy played football for a team backed by Henriques called the Oxford and St George's Under 12s football team, who had a chant of 'Boomalaka Boomalaka!'

Dan Jones published a story saying that Johnny Jacobs and Roy James broke into the 4th floor apartment in the Bernhard Baron building and stole some toys. There's also mention by Dan that Roy stole a model train and vowed to rob a train someday. Johnny went on to manage Senrab FC, which sounded as real as the idea of someone recalling, with accuracy, something a child said 80-odd years ago.

I thought Senrab was just Barnes backwards, which puts them in the category of made-up stuff with Slkcollob United and whatever it was the man from Queens Park thingy said their club used to be called. But Senrab is real, is Barnes backwards and it references a nearby street. I looked into this Dan Jones and found that he was born just 5 years after Roy and was from the same area. He's a good egg who has an MBE and worked with Amnesty International, and his work has appeared in the V&A Museum of Childhood.

I feel bad for doubting Dan now, but have dug up so many **jet-ski-powered** stories of fantasy about Roy that they make me cautious of repeating them. He is as kind to the local community as Henriques had been, albeit with a more sensitive use of language, and I have to believe his version of events. He has no story to sell, no axe to grind, no audience to impress nor does he have any fear of London's gangsters, who must know what a positive figure he is. His feels like an authentic voice.

Chapter 39 – '47, A driver and a carman

In '47 Roy's mother Violet fled her drunken, abusive husband Sid. Roy was 12 and he had an older sister, Joanna. They moved from Fulham to Whitechapel. Whitechapel appears on those maps of Victorian-era slums, where the darker the colour of ink, the more notorious the area. The East End of London, just after the war, was wrecked. They lived in the Walburgh Street area. This area would have had close-packed terraced houses, immigrant families and itinerant workers. This street today is still cobbled, a lovely throwback to its origins, but the modern buildings surrounding it look utterly miserable and it's a corner of London that has escaped gentrification.

A trip to London often highlights the stark difference between rich and poor. I'd previously met one of the protagonists in my search for the real Weasel in their private members' club in St. James, and now I'm on the Tube to a corner of Shadwell. A poster on the train says, without context, 'united against hate'. Who writes these adverts? Are we *divided* against hate? One half of us loving hate and the other half hating hate? What does it mean? Why is the DLR so confusing? Why I am lost? Probably because I'm reading all the adverts. I get off at Shadwell, more by fluke than by design, and walk to where Roy grew up on Walburgh Street. Much of the street is gone now, partially replaced by Tait Street and tower blocks. On the corner is a cash and carry and overflowing bins and complaints about rats. The cash and carry used to be a pub called the Australian Arms. It burned down in the '50s and it had a kind of playroom upstairs, where the kids would go and play with train sets.

The mind starts looking for tiny connections to Roy's reasons for wanting to escape such an environment. Trains again. Is that too simplistic? In this neighbourhood is Cable Street, where a pitched battle between fascists and anti-fascists took place in '36, and Myrtle Street, home of Jack 'Spot' Comer, known as 'King of the Underworld' and one of many gangsters who flourished here. Today, it's mostly Bangladeshi faces, Uber cab drivers, cash and carries and kids on e-scooters, and no one takes any notice of me wandering around taking it all in. I'd like to have the council stick a blue plaque on the wall to remember Roy's life here. The locals probably have higher aspirations or, more realistically, more to worry about than remembering some old crook who lived here with his mother, a lifetime ago. We'll saunter backwards (moonwalk?) into the war years now.

Roy's father was an ARP warden, which was a serious responsibility during the Blitz. This part of London had 28,000 bombs dropped on it during the Blitz and shaped the streets we see today. The houses at the end of his street were completely, totally demolished. His mother was working as a carpet repairer. Thinking of the man who we later see waterskiing in the south of France, racing at Brands Hatch, living in a huge house in the home counties, it's a million miles from the lives of his parents. As they lived in Stepney during the war, Brodie says Roy was evacuated to Ireland.

Only children with close family in the Republic of Ireland were evacuated there from England during the war, and Roy might have been one of them. His mother was born and bred in London. His father lived his life in London (occupation, 'dock labourer', says census paperwork). But somewhere, beyond the reaches of internet family trees, old newspapers and records, there's a possible link to Ireland. Roy was shipped to Ireland, missed the excitement of London and made his own way back, says Brodie. He might have been 7 years old. This meant a journey of bus, boat, train, bus and foot, back to a besieged London. Roy craved adventure. Val Pirie, on the other hand, said that Roy was evacuated to Marazion in Cornwall. She also said it in a tone that made me not want to question her.

And to the Titanic moment of his birth. It's Friday 30th August 1935 and Roy John James is born in Doneraile Street, Fulham. Friday's child is loving and giving, says the poem, somewhat missing the mark in this case.

His parents had married on 26th November 1932, a time of national hunger marches, 2.7 million people unemployed, Oswald Mosley founding the British Union of Fascists and my new favourite football team, QPR, drawing 2-2 against Merthyr Town in the cup, forcing a replay in which the 'oops won 5-1.

Sid and Violet were married at St George in the East, Cannon Street Road, Tower Hamlets, in '32. This is fairly close to Walburgh Street. She is 21, he is 24 and listed as a shop assistant. If this paragraph was a kind of mood board, there'd be pictures of King George Vee opening Lambeth Bridge, the first Mars bar made and a trade war between the UK and Ireland. Oh, and in that year, The Times newspaper used Times New Roman for the first time, beating Comic Sans by 60 years. People born around the same time as Roy were lucky to live to be 60. Roy beat this by a year. I can see why he'd want to escape this dangerous, impoverished existence. I also see a parallel with gentlemen racers who were ex-military, who sought the thrill of danger through the medium of car racing. What I cannot see is his first step.

There is no family connection to motorsport, to crime, to anything other than a likely life of ordinary drudge in an impoverished corner of a turbulent world. If this is the latest (it won't be the last) book related to the great train robbers, then it's good to look at back at the first, by Peta Fordham. I read it in the British Library, who have an original copy. She said 'they will never be of any use to anybody again' from her high horse (although she did campaign against police corruption in later life). He was a bon vivant, loved by those who knew him, people who would overlook his shortcomings in support of their friendship. Even the Comic Sans bits in the book feel plausible to me, in the end.

Skip Barber might disagree, but perhaps being a great driver and thrill seeker is in the genes. Mia Forbes Pirie was perhaps the best-qualified person to assess Roy's life, being both close to him personally and having the professional qualifications and experience to judge his character better than my scatty efforts. She explained that he would have left a note when, on a holiday in Cornwall, one of Roy's kids left the handbrake off her Beetle, which then rolled into someone else's car. And around the same time, he rammed a love rival's car with his own truck and scarpered. She said he had a sort of 'let's try and get away with this' personality and he 'never aspired to go straight'. It was in his blood. He was a thrill seeker who always seemed wealthy, but was so loved by his friends that nobody bothered to ask how, or why. Crucially, Mia said, he wanted to keep certain aspects of his life separate. Her comments have been very helpful in understanding our man, but my PC now has a virus after having googled the sex crash film thing she mentioned. Just as well we're coming to a close.

Looking at the marriage certificate I see that Sid's father, John (Roy's grandfather), was already dead by the time of John and Violet's big day. He was a 'carman', an old name given to those who drove a horse and cart. There were 50,000 of them on London's roads then, and the invention of the car was welcomed as a way of ridding the streets of the stench of horse muck. Violet's father, Walter Gurney, was also already dead by the time of her wedding day. His occupation – 'driver'. Roy would never have known these people, but they shaped him. He was the grandson of a carman and a driver.

I think driving is in your genes. Skip is as old as Roy, and still alive, and while he has lapped life much faster than me in my polystyrene helmet, I think Roy's flat-out fun is more appealing than Skip's, even with 'time served' considered. As Jan Lammers, and others, told me, Roy had an 'all-or-nothing' existence. And it's hard not to have some admiration for him turning such a drab start in life into one so spectacularly colourful. Roy said in a letter from prison to his friend Peter in '71, 'I could fill a book with my ideas.' Well Roy (I am not calling you Weasel any more, it doesn't seem right), perhaps this Amazon self-published bit of literary shonk goes some way towards that goal. Racing promoter David Mills said 'I think motor racing was his lifeline.' Val Pirie went further and said that Roy loved two things; cheating the police and getting money to go racing. She also said that Lerwick by boat in March was lovely, so make up your own mind on that one. Without any doubt, his friends loved him.

My letterbox flaps – my pursuit of Roy's real story has cost me a £180 penalty for having driven into central London recently. I can't even do that properly. But I've loved learning about Roy and sharing his story with you. The world seemingly went from horses, to cars, to extortionate public transport and traffic cameras faster than The Nigel at Silverstone. Thinking of the snotty fine, and to cheer myself up, I mark the kids bicycles page of an old Argos catalogue and post it, unstamped, to Bernie. I'll leave the last words to Roy, who once said, 'My thoughts are, first and foremost, racing.'

------ end ------

Thanks

I'd like to use an overly long sentence here to thank Roy McCarthy for the snazzy cover and Mankee Cheng for prufereedin, plus all those who joined at this book's launch event at The Motorist. This book is much saucier than it might have been thanks to David Brodie, and Peter and Shirley Procter added a depth to Roy's life than I would have otherwise missed. Mia Forbes Pirie was lovely to talk to and Val Pirie kept me on my toes; thank you, both. Thanks to Jeremy Bouckley, Jan Lammers and Nick Goozee for the racing stories. Nick Mitchell, IOU doughnuts. Thanks to Ted Wentz and Derek Warwick for the motorsport anecdotes. They won't be reading, but thanks to 'name' for the input and to 'B' for the inside stuff. I kept my word and kept schtum; please don't nail my nipsy to a fence or whatever it is gangsters do nowadays. Thanks to JayEmm on YouTube. Thanks to the many others who wished to remain nameless, to my bloody brilliant Mum and Dad, Yoko, Lucy, Bean, Claudia, Freya, Darryl Sleath, Team sLotus [sic], Phil Graden, Adam Wilkins, Jack, Gavin Big-Surname, Geoff Ames, Eric Rood, Mr Swanson, plus Mr Trotsky and Mr Taylor for your insights on the rozzers, and you, reader, for buying this book. And take a breath. If Sam James is reading this, I hope you're happy and would love to hear from you. Ta.

Legal very small print

The Author has gone to every reasonable length to ensure that the people mentioned in this book are quoted accurately, and that times, dates and actions etc. are correct BUT (note use of caps) it's entirely possible that there are errors. It is not the Author's intention to slander, defame, misquote or generally piss up the leg of anyone. The Author would be happy to correct any mistakes made in future editions. No part of this book may be reproduced or distributed in any form without prior written permission from the Author, with the exception of non-commercial uses permitted by copyright law. No part of this book may be reproduced or transmitted by any means, except as permitted by UK copyright law or the Author.

Other stuff

The Author writes for Classic Retro Modern, Absolute Lotus and other magazines, and has also published the following titles, which you'll find on Amazon.

Confessions from quality control – first hand stories of car factory cock-ups.

Nothing handles like a rental car – or 'how to get blacklisted by Hertz', European road-tripping silliness.

SUPER: Old, odd, interesting, obscure and abandoned filling stations – a series of photobooks covering different regions of the UK showing the decline of the petrol pump.

Hands up!: The real lives of puppets who used to be on the telly – 'f*cking weird', Richard Porter. A surreal thing I did.

Killer drinks: A compendium of lethal alcoholic drinks from around the world – I am very, very proud of this pocket-sized boozy fun.

About the Author

Rich von Duisberg (above, middle) lives in Leicestershire and has never, ever, vandalized the Canal Street sign. You can email him at richvonduisberg@gmail.com

ISBN - 9798876611321

Printed in Great Britain
by Amazon